"I will read your future," the old woman said slowly.

Rick scowled at her, and then shrugged. "Suit yourself."

"You do not believe?"

"I believe in what my hands make."

The old woman smiled, showing needle-sharp teeth. She got up slowly and went to the table. She lifted away a cloth and revealed a silver bowl filled with clear water.

Rick laughed, without malice.

The woman's blood-red pupils flared wide. "Time is real, Earthman, as real as this Mars you stand on and as easy to reach, once you know the way."

She bend her head over the bowl. It got quiet. The old woman's breathing rose and fell with a slow, deep rhythm. Suddenly, her crimson pupils blazed. Little red suns, burning and terrible.

She stood up, shaking. "I saw your future," she hissed. "I saw your shadow over Mars—I saw the rule of Mars to you! That is your future—if you live."

THE NEMESIS
FROM TERRA

by

LEIGH BRACKETT

ace books
A Division of Charter Communications Inc.
A GROSSET & DUNLAP COMPANY
1120 Avenue of the Americas
New York, New York 10036

THE NEMESIS FROM TERRA

Copyright ©, 1961, by Ace Books, Inc.

An ACE Book

Printed in U.S.A.

CHAPTER I

RICK stood perfectly still in the black blind notch of the doorway. The thunder of his own blood in his ears drowned any other sound, but his eyes, cold pale amber under tawny brows, watched the narrow tunnel of the street.

Three shadows came slipping through the greenish pools of moonlight on the age-worn stones.

Rick's left hand rose and steadied. Harsh echoes rolled and slammed between the packed, still rows of houses. Two of the shadows fell without a sound. The third stood upright in a shaft of Phobos-light and screamed.

Rick saw him clearly—a black anthropoid from the sea-bottom pits, one of the queer inhabitants of an evolutionary blind alley you were always running into on Mars. Some said they had once been men, and degenerated in their isolated, barren villages. Others said they were neither man nor ape, just something that got off on a road that went nowhere. Rick didn't care much. All that interested him was that the black apes were trained now like hounds to course men for the press-gangs of the Terran Exploitations Company.

Rick had no wish to slave in the Company mines until he died. He hit the black boy hard in the midriff and shut him up for good. After that, there was silence.

Rick had never heard silence like that before except on the dead worlds. The Company press-gang was beating the whole Quarter, from the stews on the Street of Nine Thousand Joys north into the angle of the city wall, but the noise they made doing it didn't seem to touch the silence of Ruh. It was like the alloy skin of a spaceship, that you couldn't touch with fire or acid or steel.

He went on, down the narrow twisting street. Doors and windows in thick walls, like gouged-out eyes. There were people behind them, all right. You could smell them. Hundreds of centuries of people, too many of them, living there. But it was like walking through the catacombs in the Terran Moon.

That was because there was a new law on Mars—a world worn threadbare and weary with the weight of time, where the little laws of the city-states had been enough since men could remember. Ed Fallon had come from earth with his Terran Exploitations Company, and now the Company was Law—at the frontiers, beyond ordinary law, making its own rules and breaking men's backs over them. The floating Terran population fought the Company when they could, feebly. The human Martians of the city-states like Ruh barred their doors and windows and prayed destruction on every alien head.

Quite suddenly Rick was up against the city wall, and there was no longer any place to go.

Back of him the crimpers were working in. On the other side of the wall, even if he could climb its enormous bulk, was a three-quarter-mile drop straight down, to the bottom of the dead sea.

Rick turned. His eyes held a green glint.

Two Martian miles away across the sea-bottom, a rocket ship went up from the Company port, slamming like a bullet into the black sky. Southward the broken towers of King City stood high over the flat roofs. A good mile beyond that, hidden in a shallow valley, was New Town, the brawling frontier gateway to half the world whence Rick had come. There were no lights anywhere.

Unseen men fought and cursed and screamed, but the silence didn't go away.

Rick settled his thick wide back against the wall and let his left hand swing free with the weight of the blaster.

Somebody yelled. They had found the dead anthropoids. Rick heard boot-heels hitting the stones, coming closer.

Quite suddenly there was light.

If he hadn't been flat against the wall he wouldn't have seen it. He realized then that the houses on the left didn't run flush to the city wall. There was a gap about two feet wide, and about twenty feet along it somebody had opened a door, a thin, dim crack.

Rick slid into the tunnel, sideways, and fast.

A woman's harsh, angry whisper snarled something in Low Martian. A squatty shadow moved across the bottom of the light. The door began to close. Rick's shoulder hit it just before the bar dropped. Something tumbled away from it with a whooshing gasp. Rick went in, kicked the door shut behind him, and dropped the bar with his right hand. The left held the blaster.

Nobody moved.

The room was cut in the thickness of the city wall. It was little. It stank. The roof touched Rick's rough, tawny head. There was a shelf bed covered with musty blankets, a table of ancient Martian work,

3

hand carved from "yrl-wood" and worth more Universal Credits than Rick could make in ten years of sweating in a glory hole, two worn matching chairs, an old woman, and a dwarf.

The dwarf was curled up in the ashes of a dead fire, gasping. He was no more than a child, thin, with green, slanting eyes. The old woman lay on the shelf bed. Rick took her for just a dirty old woman, until she looked at him.

Her eyes were like moonstones, and Rick would have believed she was blind, had he not noticed her brilliant, deep red pupils.

"Just take it easy," he said in crude Low Martian.

They said nothing. They watched him. Rick's skin crawled.

Back in the street there was noise, but he could tell that they had lost him.

He squatted down against the door. His chest heaved, and his shirt, or iridescent Venusian spider-silk, stuck to his body.

"I'm staying here until they go," he said.

The dwarf hugged his knees. His eyes burned like green coals in the smoky lantern light. The old woman didn't move or speak. From somewhere out of the tangle of blankets a small red lizard appeared and flicked down onto the dirt floor.

"I will read your future," the old woman said slowly.

Rick laughed. "I'm strapped. I got kicked off my ship for slugging the mate, and my pay is all in the pockets of girls I met afterward. If they have pockets."

"I will read your future."

He scowled at her, and then shrugged. There was no way in or out but the door at his back, and certainly nothing to fear from them physically. The noise in the street was no nearer.

"Suit yourself."

"You do not believe?" said the old woman.

"That stuff's all right for women. Me, I believe in what my hands make."

She smiled, showing needle-sharp teeth like a snake's fangs in the wrinkled dark leather of her face. Her eyes stayed on Rick, with that queer intent stare.

She got up slowly and went to the table. She lifted away a cloth and revealed a silver bowl filled with clear water.

Rick laughed, without malice.

The old woman's blood-red pupils flared wide. "You're a spaceman."

"I was born in a tramp hull, and I never been out of them since."

"The spaceship is built on a certain world. Is it chained to that world?"

"Gosh, no! What are you driving at?"

"The mind is not chained to the body, Earthman. Thought is like a ship. It can go anywhere. It can open the Gate and walk along the roads of Time. Time is real, as real as this Mars you stand on and as easy to reach, once you know the way."

Rick was scowling, his yellow eyes intent. "Maybe. But I don't believe in a future laid out for me like a treadmill. I make my own as I go along, and too many things can happen."

"Yes. But only one thing does happen. Tonight you ran away from your fellow invaders. You would have been taken for the mine gangs had not my misbegotten grandson opened the door to hear the excitement. And so, for the moment, you are safe. You came to a crossroad. You took one fork. All your possible futures stemming from that moment of choice recede onto another plane in favor of the actual one. Life, Earthman, is a series of crossroads."

"And you think you can shoot your mind up the line a-ways and sort of look over the next one?" Rick asked her.

"Yes."

Rick laughed. "Not bad. Then a guy could always know in advance which road to take, so he'd find the pot of gold and not the mud puddle."

"You still don't believe."

"I've always liked to gamble, myself. Anyway, it doesn't matter."

"No," she said slowly, "it doesn't matter."

She was looking at his face again, his hands, his eyes.

"Contradictions," she murmured, as though Rick wasn't there. "Work has made him thick and coarse, but the bones are fine. The jaw, the nose, the cheekbones, showing through the flesh as the iron ridges show under the moss of the sea-bottoms. But the mouth has yet no shape beyond self-indulgence, and the eyes—the eyes sleep!"

Rick laughed again, easily. "Is that why you want to read my future?" His muscles were relaxing. The noise in the street outside had blurred into distance again. The recent strenuous business of getting rid of his roll was catching up to him. He yawned.

He wasn't going to sleep. His mind was still on top. But he felt comfortable. The red lizard skittered across his feet suddenly like a tiny comet.

The old woman's voice had dropped to a whisper. "Perhaps," she said.

She bent her head over the water in the silver bowl.

It got quiet. The air was warm and close. The

dwarf hugged his knees in the ashes. The old woman's breathing rose and fell with a slow deep rhythm, like the breathing of the sea. The red lizard moved in silent little rushes over the stone floor, going nowhere.

Rick's mind played idly with the picture of roads stretching ahead in an infinite network. If you got onto one road, and didn't like it, why couldn't you simply cut across the hills to another?

The roads gradually took on a scarlet color. They moved and shifted. He tried to keep track of them, but they flowed around too much. His eyes began to ache. He shut them.

"Yes, this is better," he thought. "Pull down a nice dark curtain. Wake me at seven, Ma."

The weight of his own head jerking against his neck muscles brought an instinctive grab at slipping consciousness. He opened his eyes, starting half erect.

The old woman was standing by the table, still half bent over the looking-bowl. Her mouth was open, the breath going in and out snakily over her sharp teeth. She was staring at Rick.

The dwarf was on his hands and knees, motionless with fear, like a fly stuck in amber. The red lizard ran and ran and ran, with a terrible silent purpose, getting nowhere.

Rick's body felt as cold as a toad's belly in the rain. He started to get up. The crazy pattern of the lizard's movements drew Rick's attention. Yet without looking at them he could still see the old woman's eyes—whorls of pale cloud caught around a blood-red star.

"What are you trying to do?" he asked her thickly.

He tried to forget the lizard. Part of his brain was already trapped in the scarlet maze. His face twitched.

"Hypnotize me, you shriveled hag! All that bunk about the future! Hypnotize me!"

Sweat ran out of his hair. He braced his feet. His left hand rose, bringing the atom-gun up.

"You'd put me under and then throw me out to those crimps!" he accused her.

Her gaze pressed against his, beating back his strength. Her crimson pupils blazed. Little red suns, burning and terrible.

"You cannot fire, Earthman," she snarled.

He fought his own finger on the blaster's firing stud. The red lizard ran and ran, winding blood-bright threads around his mind.

Suddenly, from somewhere, the old woman caught up a knife.

The force of her thought hammered at him. "You cannot fire!" it said. "You cannot fire!"

Rick's muscles stood out like thick ropes. He sweated heavily, crying with weakness.

The old woman started across the room.

"I saw your future, Earthman," she whispered. "Your future, if you live."

She set the point of the knife against his throat. "I saw your shadow over Mars," she mumbled.

Rick's veins swelled. His face twisted into a death grin. The knife point bit. Then his finger pressed down on the firing stud.

As her face fell away from him, he could still see her eyes, burning red. He laughed, hoarsely, a beast sound without humor. Blood ran hot down his neck, but the knife had clattered to the pavement and she hadn't cut him deeply.

Rick turned. After a while he got the bar up and the door open. He went out. The cold night air shocked some of the dizziness out of his brain, but it felt sluggish in his skull like it had been stunned.

"My shadow," he whispered. "My shadow over Mars."

He went back down the street. The anthropoids still lay where he had shot them. The invulnerable silence of Ruh hung heavy in the moon-shot dark.

He began to shake suddenly with reaction. Weakness overcame him. He leaned against a wall, his chest laboring.

Four black shadows came slipping on silent paws from a side turning. He didn't hear them soon enough. Whirling around, he fired, but they were already on top of him. He went down, under a weight of sinewy bodies, beast-quick, strong, with the musky smell of the furred animal.

Rick's head cracked hard on the stones. He fought for a while, a blind instinctive thrashing of the body. Presently he became quiet.

One of the anthropoids stayed flat on the street. The other three drifted away into the silence, bearing his heavy weight with ease.

Some time later a small, hunched shadow slid out of the narrow space under the city wall and went swiftly south, toward the broken towers on the hill.

CHAPTER II

PHOBOS had set in the east. Diemos was no more than a red ember, low over the desert. The King City of Ruh lay silent under the sullen glow, its empty towers open to the wind. The moonlight was like a splashing of old blood on the stones.

Only in the lower tiers, that had been the rooms of state, the public offices, the libraries and treasure-houses, were the walls still sound. There was life there.

One flaring torch burned in the throne room, where kings of the line of Karadoc once sat, when there were salty blue seas on Mars, and green hills above them. Only the high seat and the people around it were in the light. Surrounding them was spacious, empty darkness, rustling with old flags, heavy with the ghosts of old glories, breathing out the dry sharp taint of death.

Llaw the dwarf crouched on the ceremonial rug, woven from the long bright hair of virgins whose dust had long since been blown away by wandering winds. The dwarf had been talking for a long time, half chanting, his voice ringing thin against the stone walls. His green eyes were crazy and wild in the torchlight. Suddenly he had ceased to be a child.

From the left side of the throne a woman watched him. She was not old in years, but she was ancient in pride and sorrow, as though some inner fire, banked but unquenchable, had sapped and dried her.

At the right of the throne stood a man. His tough, sinewy body was half bared in the harness of a common soldier, much worn, but his arms and accouterments were bright. His face was lean, scarred, sullen, and savage, and his eyes were the eyes of a caged wolf.

This was Beudach, chief of the fighting men of the Ruh—a warrior without a battle. His soul hung with the tattered banners in the hall. To his King he had given his heart, and his whole knowledge of harms and the way of using them. Now he watched the grandson of the seeress as a prisoner watches the turning of the key in his cell lock.

On the throne itself sat a boy.

He was dark, and bright, and beautiful. He was like a swordblade, or a new spear, and the fire that smoldered in his mother blazed in him. He was Haral, last of the line of Karadoc, with the plain, ancient iron Collar of Ruh locked proudly on his young throat.

Llaw the dwarf stopped speaking.

For a while there was silence. Then Haral spoke.

"His shadow over Mars," he said slowly.

"My grandmother saw it, Lord," insisted the dwarf. "She was a great seeress."

"The Rule of Mars to an Earthman," mused Haral. "The outland yoke hammered on our necks to stay."

The woman cried out, but the wolf-faced man was before her, bending over the throne.

"Now, Lord! Now is the time to strike, if there's any blood or pride left in the men of Mars!"

The boy rose, slowly. The torchlight crimsoned his white skin.

"Beudach."

The wolf-faced man dropped to one knee. "Send Parras to me."

Beudach went away, smiling.

"Do you know where this Earthman is?" Haral asked Llaw.

"No, Lord. But I will find him." He licked his lips. "There is a blood debt."

"It shall be paid."

The woman set her hands on the arm of the high seat and laughed, once, silently.

Beudach returned. There was a man with him, a

plump, smiling, youngish man in a sky-blue robe. His eyes were like those of the dead seeress, moonstones flecked with red.

"I want word given to the leaders of every city that pays seizin to Ruh," Haral said to him. "Say that the old Banner of the Twin Moons is raised again, this time against the tyrants of Earth. Tell them to gather what strength they can, and hold it in readiness, and to send their chief warriors here to Ruh, secretly, for a council of war. Llaw!"

The dwarf sprang up.

"Go with Parras. Give him the description of this Earthman, Rick, so that he can warn the cities to watch for him. Then go yourself and spread the word through Ruh."

Llaw and Parras bowed and started out. Haral stopped them.

"Wait. You must give them a slogan." He laughed, boylike, his face aglow with excitement. "Give them the old one, the oldest one on Mars—the cry of the sailors and the sea-board men when the oceans rose out of their beds, and after that the cry of the people who live in the deserts and the wastes where the seas were. Tell them, Parras— 'The wind is rising!' "

The dwarf and the seer went out. Haral sprang down from the high seat. He caught his mother and whirled her around and kissed her, and then pulled Beudach's sword from the scabbard behind his left shoulder.

He shouted and threw it high in the air. The blade turned over and over in the torchlight, hurling red sparks at the darkness, and fell. Haral caught it deftly by the hilt.

Beudach watched him. There were tears in his eyes.

Ten days later Ed Fallon, head of the Company, was standing at his high window, gazing out at the vast panorama of Mars. He heard the door of his office open, but he didn't turn his head. He didn't have to. Only Jaffa Storm's tread had that particular strong, uneven rhythm.

"Come over here," Fallon said. "By gosh, it's worth looking at."

Storm put down his sheaf of reports on Fallon's desk and went over to the wide glassite window. He was a big man, nearly seven inches over six feet, with a body like a gladiator's under his black, close-fitting coverall, and his slight limp gave no impression of weakness. There was a 'Mickey' holstered on his lean hip.

He stood beside Fallon, dwarfing even his thick-chested, powerful build. He said nothing, but his black eyes saw everything with a sombre, rather terrible thoroughness.

"My baby," said Fallon. He struck his red-haired hands together and laughed. "She's growing up, Jaffa. Pretty soon she'll have all of Mars to play with."

His eyes had sparks in them, watching the surging strength of his baby—the Terran Exploitations Company, called simply, the Company.

Fallon's office was on the top floor of the Administration Pylon. It was walled with glassite, and gave a full-circle view of the Company world—laboratories, processing division, foundries, forges, tool shops, the vast pit-head housings with their train sheds, and beyond them, far enough away to be safe from the rocket-blasts, the Company spaceport, whence the cargoes of Fallonite went Earthward.

Apart from all these, behind charged walls of

13

metalloy, where the barracks where the Company work-gangs lived, while they lived.

The pylon was high enough to show other things, too. The seabottom, spreading away into pale distance under the Martian sun, its gaunt ribs showing naked through the blue-gray moss. And to the south, the Old City of Ruh, like the broken crown of a dead king dropped and forgotten on its soaring crag.

Death was out there. Age and cessation. Fallon thought no more of it than he did of last year's worn-out shoes. He watched the life of his Company, the thunder and sweat and surge of machinery and the men who bossed it, and it was his own life, his own blood and sweat and surging energy.

Young, that baby, like Earth's intrusion onto dying Mars, but already stretching out muscular hands to close around a planet. A planet whose central government was no more than a feeble token, with the real power scattered wide among the city-states still clinging to the deserts and the sea-bottoms and the barren hills. A planet practically untouched by outland hands until the discovery of Fallonite. It was disunited, ingrown, weak, an easy touch for the first strong man who could see wealth and power springing out of its fallow fields.

"By gosh," said Fallon again, softly, "it's worth looking at."

"Yes," said Storm, also softly. He limped over and sprawled his huge length onto a couch, pulling cigarets from his breast pocket. His thick hair was blacker than his coverall, his skin hardly lighter. He was Terro-Mercurian, born and bred in the blazing, thundering valleys of the Twilight Belt, where legend had it that the babies came with horns and tails, and with all the heart burned out of them with the heat.

Fallon turned back to his desk, looking with distaste at the stack of papers.

"Bah! I'd rather be back in the foundry than mess with this stuff."

"You're a liar," said Storm. "You're a conniving, crafty old fox, and you love it. You never were a laboring man at heart, anyway."

Fallon looked at him. He decided to laugh.

"You're not a comfortable guy to have around." He sat down. "How you coming with those new men?"

"Like always. There's one big yellow-eyed devil I may have to kill. I hope not. He's strong as a horse."

Fallon chuckled. "Nothing like a cheap labor supply! And as long as I pull the strings that make the New Town go, it'll be jammed with the best supply there is—floaters, homesteaders, placer men, spacehands, bums—guys who can vanish with no kicks but their own."

"Until the law moves in."

Fallon roared with mirth. "Yeah! That worries me a lot!"

"Uh huh. Just the same, I hope they don't get leery about going into the Old City. I'd rather take 'em there. Not so tough on our men. The Marshies just sit tight and hope we'll kill each other off. In the New Town, they don't like crimpers." Fallon shrugged. "That's your worry, Jaffa. Just keep those pits open, that's all I want."

"You'll get what you want."

Fallon nodded. He sweated over the papers for a time in silence. Storm sat still, smoking. Outside, the Company hurled its rude and alien noise against the quiet of Mars.

Presently Storm spoke. "I was in Ruh last night. Old Ruh."

"Have a good time?"

"Fallon, I smell trouble."

The red-haired man looked up. "Trouble?"

"The city feels different. It has felt different, since that last raid ten days ago."

"What the devil! Are you going psychic on me? The Marshies won't even say good morning to us. And besides, those ancient, washed-out little twerps wouldn't have the getup to make trouble."

"Listen, Fallon." Storm leaned forward. "I spent four seasons in the cliff-caves of Arianrhod, down on the edge of Darkside. The people aren't human, but they know things, and I learned a few of them."

His dark face twitched slightly. "I walked through Ruh last night, and I felt it, through the walls and the darkness and the silence. There's a new feeling in the people. Fear, restlessness, a peculiar urgency. I don't know why, yet, or what it will lead to. But there's a new thing being whispered back of those closed doors. They're telling each other 'The wind is rising!' "

His sombre black gaze held Fallon. After a while, in the stillness, Fallon repeated the phrase.

"The wind is rising."

He laughed suddenly. "Well, let it! It'll take a bigger wind than any old Mars has left to blow my walls down!"

The telescreen hummed, calling for attention. Fallon flipped the connection.

"Kahora calling—Mr. Hugh St. John," the operator said.

"Put him through." Fallon winked broadly at

16

Storm and then composed his face to a friendly smile. The screen flickered and cleared.

"Hello, Fallon," Hugh St. John said. "Are you busy?"

"Not for you. What's on your mind?"

"Mind? I'm beginning to wonder if I have one!" St. John's sensitive, aquiline face looked tired and discouraged. He had untidy fair hair and blue eyes that were unexpectedly shrewd and penetrating.

"Things not going so well, huh?" Fallon said.

St. John laughed bitterly. "The whole purpose of the Unionist movement is to promote understanding between Earthmen and the Martians, so that each can give his best to the other without hurting either. And what have we done so far? We've caused a complete break between the Pan-Martians and the Moderates, and the feeling between our two races get worse every day. No, Fallon. Things are not going so well."

"Are there any new rumors of—well, trouble? Rioting, let's say?"

"We have contact now only with the Moderates, and there aren't many of them, as you know. They're shunned as bitterly as we are. And of course here in Kahora we don't know much about the Outside. You know what a Trade City's like. I should think you'd have more chance of hearing than we."

"There's nothing that I know of," Fallon said innocently. "Look here—you need more money?"

St. John nodded. "Well, if we could carry on our work in the Polar cities, there's a bare chance. The Thinkers are revered all over Mars, and if we could win them over they might swing native opinion our way. But you've already given so much it seems wasteful."

"I still got plenty. How much?"

"Well, about five thousand U.C.'s ought to be about right."

"Make it six, and let me know when you need more. I'll send the draft through right away."

St. John's eyes glowed mistily. "Fallon, I don't know what we'd do without you!"

"I'm not giving away anything. Mars means as much to me as it does to you." Fallon raised his hand. "So long pal."

"Good by. And thanks."

The screen went dead. Fallon leaned back in his chair and grinned.

"The fool," he said. "The dear, sweet, lily-livered fool!"

Storm watched him with faint amusement. "Sure of that?"

"What do you mean?" snapped Fallon. "I've brought that Union Party up practically by hand. Give them something to focus their opinions on, and they start tearing each other's heads off in no time, never knowing it's what I want them to do."

Storm shrugged. "I wonder?" he said.

"By heavens, Jaffa, you're so suspicious I wonder you trust yourself."

"I don't," said Storm quietly. "That's why I've stayed alive."

Fallon stared at him. And then, for the second time, the telescreen hummed—emitting a series of short, nervous sounds. The "urgent" signal.

Both men went to it, quickly. The screen sprang to life. A man in greasy coveralls leaned forward as though he were trying to come through physically. There was blood running down his face.

"Trouble in Number Five drift. That new gang has gone wild."

"How bad is it?" demanded Fallon, his tones sharp, hoarse.

"They took the guards. Beat 'em down with their shackle chains. That big guy Rick, he's leading them. After grabbing four Mickeys, they dug in behind some ore cars, and they got four Mickeys."

"A Mickey never gave you that."

The man wiped blood off his face with his fingers. "They're throwing ore fragments. My guess is they'll make a rush for the shaft."

"Very well, I'll be right down." Fallon killed the screen and turned to his companion. "How many men in that gang, Jaffa?"

"Thirty-two."

Fallon made another connection and spoke briefly to the huge white Venusian on the visaplate. The picture showed racks of arms and other huge men in the background. It had been Jaffa Storm's idea to have an all-Venusian corps of Middle-Swampers for his strong-arm work. Being outlanders and fairly savage, they had interest in two things only—food and fighting. Storm saw to it they had plenty of both.

"Vargo send fifteen men down to Number Five drift," Fallon said. "Take a high-power Banning shocker. There's thirty-two guys down there want to play rough, and they're all yours!"

CHAPTER III

MAYO MCCALL looked down through the glassite wall of her booth ten feet above the floor of Number Five drift. Thirty feet to her right was the shaft where the Fallonite ore went up to the surface. To her left was the brilliantly-illuminated tunnel that followed the vein out under the waste of the dead sea-bottom.

Mayo McCall watched the men running back and forth below. Quite calmly she reached out and closed the switch that controlled her testing beam—the ray that spanned the head of the drift and checked every carload of dull red rock for Fallonite content, the chemically amorphous substance that was already beginning to revolutionize the Terran plastic industry.

Mayo was alone. No one on the drift floor was paying any attention to her. She folded her arms on the table in front of her and peeled back the sleeve of her dark green technician's overall. She pressed a hidden stud on her wristwatch.

The lens and half the silver case rose, revealing a microscopic two-way radio. Mayo counted five slowly, watching the men below. Her brown eyes held a deep glow. She had a strong, supple body whose curves even the coverall couldn't hide, and hair of a rich, warm mahogany color that made her skin look like cream.

"Go ahead," the radio whispered.

Softly, distinctly, without moving her lips, Mayo McCall spoke.

"There's trouble with a new gang, here in my drift.

Set the amplifiers and recorders. I'm going down . . . Wait. A bunch of Venusian guards just arrived with a Banning shocker. This looks big. It may be just what we've wanted."

"Be careful, Mayo. You know what they'll do if they discover what you're doing."

"I know. There goes Fallon and Jaffa Storm. This ought to be good. Stay with me."

She pulled her sleeve down carefully. The loose cloth covered the radio. She opened the door of the booth.

The drift was empty now for as far as she could see. She went quickly down the plastic steps and turned left, going silently and keeping close to the red rock wall. The rails of the dilly road glinted burnished silver in the white glare.

From up ahead, around a bend in the tunnel, came the sudden brittle whine of a heavy-duty shocker cutting in.

The first beam was low power. Crouched behind an ore car, Rick felt the shock run through him like liquid fire. It made his heart pound, but the pain wasn't too much to take.

There were twenty-two men spread out beside him along the rail. The other nine had been put to sleep with the Mickey shockguns of the guards, in the first scrimmage. The focus of the Banning was widened to take in the lot.

"Jimminy! We can't take that!" one of the men cried shrilly. "They'll step up the power."

"Shut up," Rick told him. The Venusian, Vargo, called to them. He looked innocent and happy, incongruously like a nice old lady with the dead-white hair coiled high on his head.

"You come out now, eh?" he said to the miners.

21

No answer. Vargo looked around. Jaffa Storm had just come up, running easily with his odd, limping stride. Fallon was some distance behind him. Fallon waved his hand.

"It's your show, boys!" he shouted.

He stopped, not too close, and lounged against the wall.

"Advance your power at the rate of one notch per second," Storm said quietly. The Venusian with the Banning grinned and took hold of the small lever. "I will count to ten," Storm said clearly, to no one in particular.

It grew very still under the cold brilliance. Rick peered around a wheel. The manacles clashed softly as he raised the Mickey in his twitching, jerking hand.

He didn't fire. The little guns had a shorter range than the distance a strong man could throw an ore fragment, which was why the rebels still had opposition. The Company men moved back beyond the ore fragments.

Rick watched the lever click forward on the Banning. Little blue lights began to flicker on the rim of the wheel in front of him. His body began to jerk with the same erratic violence. Each separate nerve stood out in coruscating agony.

Jaffa Storm began to count.

Jaffa Storm's voice echoed under the stone vault with the rhythmic impersonality of a clock tolling.

When he said, "Five," one of the rebel miners began to scream.

"I'm coming out!" he shrieked. "I'm coming out!" Jaffa Storm stopped counting. He held his hand out, flat. The current stayed level. In the dead silence the man crawled across the rock, his shadow black and inhuman beneath him. His wristchains dragged, clashing.

Six others followed. Rick watched them. Once he tried to raise the Mickey, but his hand was like an old man's, palsied and without strength.

Storm began to count again.

Three times the advancing level was stopped while men crawled and whimpered across the rock. When Storm said, "Ten," there was only one man left beside Rick. He must have had a weak heart. He was dead.

"Cut your power," Storm said.

The Venusian looked surprised, but he thumbed the stud. The whining stopped. Rick's body went lax. He lay face down, breathing in hoarse animal gasps. Sweat lay like thick oil on his skin.

"Rick," Storm said. "Are you ready to quit?"

After a long while Rick laughed.

"I suppose," said Storm, "you think I'll kill you anyway."

Rick's words had no shape to them, but their meaning was plain.

Storm nodded. He gestured to the Venusian. The man got up, and Storm sat down behind the Banning.

The guards and the dough-faced exhausted men moved back, against the wall. They didn't speak. Their breathing sounded harsh and loud. A still white glare filled the drift.

Storm lighted a cigarette, without haste. He placed matches in the pack, weighted it, and threw it. He didn't appear to strain at all, but the pack struck the wall behind Rick with audible force.

Presently Rick got his knees under him. He picked

up the cigarette and sat back against the rock, dragging smoke deep into his lungs. It was quiet enough so that the faint sizzling of the illuminating tube sounded very loud. Rick looked up at it.

It was sunk in a trough in the ceiling and protected with heavy wire screen. There was no way to break it. Rick knew that. He'd already tried every way there was. The main switch for the whole length of the tube was back near the mouth of the drift. There were also switches for the individual sections, but they were not within his reach.

He sat almost at the peak of an oblique bend in the drift. To his left the tunnel ran into a dead end, without side galleries or even cover of any kind. Most of it, because the bend was shallow, was in clear range of the Banning.

Almost directly in front of him, in the opposite wall, was the dark opening of an abandoned side gallery. It probably led into a cul-de-sac, although it might, just possible, cut into one of those endless mazes left by the giant mud-worms of prehistoric Mars, whose tunnelings remain fossilized under the sea-bottoms. In either case, it would mean only the difference between a fast death and a slow one, and as for reaching it, it might as well have been on Phobos.

Off to his right, across the naked, pitiless stone, Jaffa Storm dropped his cigarette and stepped on it.

He leaned forward. His hands touched the Banning with gentle delicacy. He tilted the muzzle high and flashed an experimental beam. This time the focus was tight, the power-whine hysterically high.

A thin stream of pale and crackling fire licked out, touched the opposite wall, and was gone. The smoking surface was fused like glass.

Quite suddenly one of the chained men turned his face to the wall and began to vomit.

Rick crouched down behind a metal wheel. His yellow eyes had the cold cruelty of those of a cat. His body was relaxed and still.

Jaffa Storm leveled the Banning, his dark face betraying neither pleasure nor interest.

He laid the beam on the disc of Rick's wheel and let it stay.

The nearness of the charge sent fire shocking through Rick's flesh. The wheel began to heat. Blue flames danced on its rim. Sweat poured down Rick's face, and dried, and the skin reddened angrily. His eyes were tortured.

He sprang suddenly, sideways along the rail, toward another wheel. The beam flicked over his head and came down ahead of him. He leaped back, making a dash the other way. Again the beam was quicker.

He dropped behind the wheel again. The beam found the disc and stayed.

Rick measured the distance to the gallery opening. He laughed silently, without humor, and gathered himself.

From the empty drift, beyond Storm and the men and the Venusian guards, beyond Ed Fallon, leaning white-faced against the wall, came a woman's voice.

"Stop!" it said.

Hasty footsteps rang against the tunnel vault. Voices broke loose in a nervous babble. The heat and the blue fire went away from the wheel. Rick looked around it, cautiously.

He saw the girl and she was beautiful. Even in that technician's coverall she made a lovely picture as she hastened to Jaffa Storm. Her hair clung in deep sorrel curls around her face, her brown eyes were blazing. She was so full of fury that she actually seemed to give off light.

"Stop that," she said. "Stop it!"

Fallon was coming up behind her. He looked rather sick.

"I've stopped," said Storm, mildly.

"It isn't enough for you to take these men off the free streets and chain them up and make slaves of them. You have to murder them, too!"

Storm rose lazily, motioning the Venusian back to the Banning.

"Do I do all those things, Miss?"

"Don't try to be funny! You know it's the truth."

"How do you know I do?"

"Everybody knows it!"

"Do they. Do they really." Storm's hand shot out so quickly that it was only a blurred flash. He pulled her close and said with friendly curiosity, "Or are you just trying to make me admit it, perhaps for someone else to hear?"

His free hand went over her with impersonal swiftness. She struggled, striking at him with her left arm. He laughed. He caught her wrist, and there was a faint snap of metal. He held her tight and peeled the sleeve back.

"Yes," he said. "Yes, I thought so."

He stripped off the watch-radio and crushed it under his heel.

Fallon whistled softly. "I better take her up to the office."

Storm nodded. His black eyes were warm. The girl lay quiet in his arms. The neck of her dark-green coverall had been torn open, and her throat and cheeks were smooth like new cream.

"You're awfully strong," she whispered. She shivered and let her head roll back against him. Her eyes were closed. "I guess I'm caught."

"M-m-mh."

"Are you going to kill me?" she asked him.

"That might depend."

She raised her lashes. "I don't think I want to die yet."

He laughed. He held her off, facing him, so he could look into her eyes.

"That's awfully quick work, baby."

"Time doesn't mean much in a spot like this."

"You're a liar, precious. A most beautiful, lovely liar."

She said nothing. Her lips were warm, rosy and alive.

"I can read your mind," Storm said.

"You're awfully smart," she murmured. "Because I can't read it myself."

Storm laughed again, softly. He bent his towering height and kissed her, taking his time.

In the middle of it, with her mouth still pressing his, she brought her knee up, hard, wth deadly accuracy.

Rick shouted. Jaffa Storm doubled up, his face twisted with stunned agony. The girl kicked him again, on the knee, and broke free.

"I've trained my mind, too," she yelled, and ran.

The Venusians burst into a sudden raucous howl of laughter at Storm, who was huddled over on his knees, retching. The manacled men joined in.

Fallon made a grab for the girl. He missed, but

some of the guards ran out and her back to the shaft was barred. From behind the ore car Rick bellowed.

"The light switch!"

Her gaze flicked from him to the switch near the tunnel mouth, all in the instant between one step and the next. The switch was on the opposite wall, away from the guards. She moved.

"Don't fire!" Fallon yelled. "I want her alive." He began to run, with half a dozen big Middle-swampers loping past him. The girl was going like a dark-green comet.

Jaffa Storm got up. He kept his body bent, but his feet were steadier than Rick knew his would have been. There was no expression on his face, not even pain. He struck the Venusian away from the Banning. He laid him out cold, and never glanced at the body. He fired. His beam went between two Venusians, close enough to singe them, and hit the wall five feet to the girl's left. She didn't falter.

"Stop that!" Fallon yelled furiously. "She's got to be questioned!"

Storm fired again. The Venusians had scattered out of the way. The girl dropped flat, rolling. The beam missed her by the minimum margin, and then Rick was on his feet, running fast across the stone pathway.

He shouted. Storm's attention wavered slightly. Without breaking stride, Rick threw what was in his left hand.

It was an ore fragment. It was heavy, and jagged. It took Storm across the left side of his face and knocked him flat.

The light went out.

The Banning was still on. Its beam made an eerie unreal shimmer in the blackness. Rick's eyes adjusted quickly. He was heading for the tunnel mouth before Storm hit the ground, and in the bluish glimmer he made out the girl's shadow, racing for the same place. Elsewhere, pandemonium was on a holiday.

Nobody chased them. They were afraid of the Banning. There was a heaving and profane commotion back against the wall. Somebody got hold of the Banning finally and screamed, "Watch out!" and started to flash the beam around. Rick and the girl collided at the tunnel mouth and fell. The tongue of flame licked the air, crackling, where their heads had been, and flashed past. Before it could come back they had plunged into the pitch darkness of the gallery.

It turned. They crashed the blind wall and clawed around the corner, and behind them the Banning beam hit the rock and chewed away in a baffled fury.

"Come on," Rick said.

They went, faster than any sane people would have dared. They fought the rock walls and the trash of abandoned digging on the ground, the darkness, and themselves.

Three times Rick thought, "This is it. End of the tunnel. Dead end!" Then his groping hands would slide around a corner, and they'd go on.

Suddenly, quite suddenly, the drift changed. The floor was round, like a huge pipe, instead of level. There was no debris. The walls were curved, with a curious regular smoothness under the hand.

After a while they slowed, and then stopped. The silence lay as dead and heavy as the darkness. Their hoarse breathing had a quality of sacrilege, like noise in a tomb.

Instinctively they moved close together, close enough to touch. Rick's wrist-chains clashed softly.

"They haven't followed," the girl whispered.

"No. They'll send the black boys. The anthropoids."

Silence. Blood drumming hot behind their ears.

"We're in one of those mazes I've heard about, aren't we?" the girl murmured. "Where the big worms used to crawl before the sea-bottoms hardened."

"That's right."

"Is there any way out?"

"I don't know. Sometimes worm tunnels lead into a pit, or a cliff face. Sometimes the roof has been cracked. About this one, I don't know."

"Not a very good chance, is it?" But her voice showed no fear.

"I wouldn't give odds."

Silence. Their breathing, their body heat, their fear, mingling in the thick dark.

"What's your name?" Rick asked the girl.

"Mayo McCall. What's yours?"

"Richard Gunn Urquhart, but Rick's enough."

"Hello, Rick."

"Hello, Mayo." He found her shoulder and shook it. "You have courage, baby. Ha, I hope you ruined that big scut for life."

"That rock of yours didn't do him any good."

"I got a hunch it didn't finish him," said Rick. "I hope it didn't. I'd like to see that guy again, some day."

"And Fallon?" she asked him.

"Fallon and the whole blasted Company," Rick's voice was vicious. "I'd like to boot them clean to . . ."

After a while Mayo whispered, "Maybe you could, if we're lucky," Mayo whispered, after a while.

"What do you mean?" asked Rick. "Go on, explain."

"If we live, I might show you how," said the girl. "We'd better go now. Which way?"

"Which wrist am I holding?"

She moved it slightly. "The left."

"That's the way we go, then. And baby, you better be lucky!"

CHAPTER IV

WIND moved sighing through the broken walls, and the dusk came down to join it. Far out across the western wastes Phobos rode the last pale glow of the sun edging the rim of Mars. Ruh lay silent, barred and shuttered, but not asleep.

With night shadows crept through the streets. Some of them came drifting in through secret portals in the city wall and then sought the heights of the King City, where they vanished. Upon entering the flaring torchlight in the throneroom, however, they became men.

Fighting men. Of different ages, sizes, coloring, in the harness of different city-states, but all alike in one thing—the look they bore. The look of wolves in a cage.

They sat around a table of blood-red wood worn hollow by the arms of centuries of warchiefs. Haral the boy king, leaned forward like a bent blade from his high seat, and the eyes of Beudach, who stood always at his right hand, were as steel in the fire.

Only one shadow remained in the Quarters. It was small and hunched and swift-moving, and its eyes burned emerald in the Phobos-light. It went from door to door, whispering, asking, and the name it said was "Rick."

High up against the stars, in the ruined Tower of Destiny, Parras, the Seer, bent his fresh young face above his looking bowl. His mend reached out across the sea-bottoms, the sand deserts, the age-worn hills. It touched other minds, asking, and the name it said was "Rick."

To the green-eyed shadow and the mind of the seer came an unvarying answer.

"Not yet."

"Wait, then," Parras would tell them. "Keep watching. There is a blood debt to be paid. 'The wind is rising!' "

Down in the mine gallery, Rick put his hand on Mayo's shoulder. "Hold it," he cautioned the girl. "I thought I heard something."

They stood still. Presently Rick heard the noises quite clearly, somewhere far behind them in the stale blackness of the wormbore. The soft scrambling noises of many creatures, running.

"What'll we do?" Mayo asked.

"Keep going, I guess. I've only got one Mickey, and that won't even slow 'em down. Tired?"

"I'm all right. What happens when they catch us?"

"Ask me then."

They went on again. The going was fairly easy, the floor smooth and the turns gradual. Rick knew they must have left their original bore long ago, branching off into only the stars knew how many intersecting tunnels. He had no idea how long they had been wandering, only that it was too long. They simply kept going because there was nothing else to do.

The anthropoids, fresh and running easily by scent, drew closer by the minute. Rick hung back a little, behind the girl.

Quite suddenly Mayo gave a strangled cry and fell heavily. There was a dry sound of something splitting. Rick tried to stop, tripped, and went sprawling.

There was a smoothly serrated surface under him. It tapered upward, widening to the sides. He scrambled up and followed it, with Mayo beside him.

"The tunnel's blocked," she gasped. "Rick, it's blocked!"

"Sure. Here, climb up." He pulled her onto the top of the obstruction and began to crawl. Presently his head hit the roof. He reached out, groping. The obstruction curved into the side of the bore, sealing it completely.

Rick let his breath out, hard. He lay still, utterly relaxed, and listened to his heart. It was like thunder. The sweat felt cold on his skin. Mayo lay beside him, breathing unevenly.

Behind them, another sound grew louder, closing in.

After a while Rick pushed himself backward and turned around. He got the Mickey in his hand and sat waiting. His body was like lead. He slid his right hand out the length of the chain and found the girl's slender palm.

She gripped his fingers, and her grasp was cold, like ice. They sat listening to the soft rushing footsteps.

Suddenly she spoke, rather loudly. "What is this thing, Rick?"

"Don't know." He ran his knuckles over the smooth serrations. "Hey! Yes I do, too! It's the guy that built this tunnel—the old crawler himself. He died here, and turned to stone."

He laughed, not because it was particularly funny. He gave the fossil a crack with the barrel of the Mickey.

It rang hollow.

Rick hit it again, harder, and then he remembered the brittle cracking sound when Mayo fell. He got up on his knees, balled his fists together, and struck down with all his strength.

It nearly jarred his teeth out, but he knew. "Oh, cracky!" he whispered. "If I only had a pick, or a big maul!" He laughed again, sharply. He slid the heavy manacles as far down as they would go on his hands, wrapped the chain around them, and went to work.

He had a crack started when the anthropoids began to swarm up over the slope of the worm's tail.

Mayo took the Mickey. Rick went on pounding. They were so far back in the cleft between the fossil and the roof that the brutes had to come at them from the front only, and not many at a time. Mayo did all right with the Mickey, for a while. The shock-charge put the leading anthropoids to sleep, and their bodies rolled back to trip the ones coming up behind them. It was a blind fight. The blackness was choked with the sound of feet and moving bodies, and a rank animal smell. The anthropoids worked silently.

Rick drowned everything else with the smashing thunder of his manacles on the echoing stone.

"The Mickey's dead, Rick," Mayo reported at last. "The charge is gone."

"Come here. I've made a hole." She found it. "Can you break the edges back?"

"I think so." He heard her kicking, beating and straining. Things snapped. Anthropoid paws found his leg and pulled him backward. He swung. He didn't have hands any more, only a numb mass bound together with metal. The mass hit something, and for the first time there was a scream.

"It's coming!" Rick heard Mayo say.

He swung again. The blackness was full of bodies. Every time Rick swung he hit something. There was a new smell, warm and dank and sweetish. His arms were wet.

There were too many bodies. They weighed him down. He went on swinging until his arms were held tight. He kicked. Things smashed and fell away from his boots, but they came back again. Presently his legs were held, too. He heaved and twisted. Some of the paws were shaken loose. For a moment he was almost free. He got in a few good ones, and then he was down again. From a great distance Mayo's voice was calling out.

"Rick! Rick, come on!" it said.

He tried it, but it was no good. And then suddenly a cyclone hit the heaving mass on top of him, and there were gaps in the paws that held him. Mayo screamed and tugged at him.

He used strength which he didn't know he had left, to thrash free. Mayo plunged down the hole, dragging his feet after her. An anthropoid grappled with him. He slugged it with his irons and dropped through into the inside of the fossil worm. Two of the brutes tried to get through the hole at once and jammed there.

Mayo helped him up and they staggered away down the worm's interior.

They were knee deep in dust. The intestinal structure had fallen away, crumbled, and dried, while the outer shell hardened. The clouds that rose behind them slowed the anthropoids. Rick and Mayo went on, far beyond their physical strength driven by a raw, primitive urge for survival.

It came to Rick dimly, after a while, that something was happening.

"Falling in," he said thickly. "Vibration—cracking it."

It was horrible in the dark. Smothering dust, the noise of splitting destruction everywhere. Parts of the shell had become homogenous with the hardened mud, and apparently that was caving in, too. The miners always feared the treacherous strata away from the true rock that held the ore veins.

There were screams again behind them.

"When we reach the head there won't be any place to go," Mayo said suddenly. "Solid rock."

The cracking ran forward over their heads. A falling mass grazed Rick's shoulder. He pushed the girl on faster. Dust rolled strangling against their lungs. There was a terrible, crushing, bottled-up thunder.

Their heads struck the top abruptly. They dropped, crawling. The space narrowed in on them. The dust thickened. Mayo whimpered hoarsely. There was ripping, splitting crash!

Dead end . . .

Several days later, Hugh St. John was standing on the terrace of his apartment, well up in the tallest building in Kahora, the Trade City for Mars. His sensitive young face was drawn and grim. He nervously was smoking a slender Venusian cigarette.

Kahora was halfway around the planet from Ruh and Fallon's Company. It was night. Diemos rode low in the purple-black sky above the glassite dome that covered the city, shielding its polyglot inhabitants from the naked weather of Mars.

Down below, the streets of Kahora lay like a little web of jewels. St. John listened to the city's pulse. It was a slow, quiet beat. The business that went on here was the sterile handling of things already made and done, figures added up by sleek men who spent their idle hours in the Dream Palace and the exotic night clubs. Even the air was artificial, carefully cleaned, scented, and kept at an even temperature.

He had been in Vhia, the Trade City for Venus. That hadn't been so bad. Venus was a young planet, lusty and strong. Even the glassite dome hadn't been able to keep out the savage beat of the rains and the sense of hot jungle just outside. Men were busy there, too, the heart and brain of the commerce of a thrusting, aggressive world. Where there was enmity with the Venusians, it had been a healthy one.

Here everything was old, passive, faded and worn out. Even the Martian hatred of the Earthmen, the invaders, was a silent thing, festering in barren darkness. The stream of Martian trade flowed through Kahora like the chilling blood of an old man already three-quarters dead.

St. John's mouth twisted bitterly. The only living thing on Mars was Ed Fallon and his alter ego, the Company. Alive, he thought, like an evil beast—hungry, independent, and fatal.

Presently the robot servant at the door identified and admitted the man St. John had been waiting for.

"Mak," St. John cried. "Mak, did you find out anything?"

Eran Mak shook his head. He was Martian, a Low-canaler from over Jekkara way, and he looked like what he was—a civilized bandit. The dubious fame of his people went as far back into Martian history as the history tself. He was small, tough and wiry, with a slender dark face, a friendly smile, and eyes like drops of hot gold. He wore a cluster of tiny bells in his left ear, and his clothing, the fashionable white tunic of the Trade Cities, gave him the satanic look.

"I'm afraid there's not much hope, Hugh," he said quietly. "I finally made connections with Christy. Since they found out about Mayo, he's scared green. She and this fellow Rick got away all right, into an abandoned drift, but heaven only knows what happened after that. Christy says they sent the black boys after them, and only a few came back. Some of them were all messed up—crushed arms and such, as though they'd been caught in a cave-in. So I guess they're both done for."

He lifted his lean shoulders. St. John turned away.

"Were you in love with her, Hugh?" Eran Mak was one of the few who could venture to ask such a question. He was St. John's best friend.

"I don't know. I don't think I could have sent her there if I had been in love with her. And yet, when I knew she was caught, and her radio suddenly stopped sending, my heart turned to ice." Suddenly he shivered. "Mak, if she's dead, then I killed her!"

"She knew what she was doing," Mak consoled him.

St. John shuddered again. He sat down and put his face in his hands.

Eran Mak crossed the terrace and also seated himself, the little bells tinkling faintly as he moved. He smoked a cigarette in silence. Then he frowned.

"This is going to make Fallon awfully suspcious," he said.

St. John drew a long breath. "That's true. Well, I'll stall him as long as I can. Anyway, I cashed his last draft!" He rose abruptly. "I don't know how we can manage to continue the work without the rat's money."

"It may not matter. There's a storm brewing, Hugh. One devil of a big thundering storm. It's all under cover, but here and there a little puff of breeze warns of a gathering tornado. It may blow us all clean off Mars."

"And this world's last chance for life will be gone. I've failed, Mak. My whole plan has been a fool's dream from the beginning."

He gripped the rail of the terrace, looking out over the jewelled city.

"Think what we could give them, Mak, if they'd only let us! The strength, the new ideas, the new roads to travel! But they won't allow it. They slam their doors in our faces, and the Martian Planetary Government only refrains from kicking us off into space because they don't want open trouble with Earth and Venus.

"Only Ed Fallon gets anywhere. He's going to own all Mars in a few years, because of that cursed ore he discovered. Money will make such a big noise in the Government's ears that any yelling the people do won't amount to a penny whistle in a hurricane. And Mars will be just as dead, either way it goes."

He hit the rail hard with his hand and started pacing.

"My only chance of getting rid of Fallon failed

when Mayo was caught before she could get proof of what he and Storm are doing. With that, I might have gone to the Interplanetary Coordination Authority—their Labor Board would have made an investigation. But now it's too late!"

He sat down again.

Eran Mak set the tiny bells chiming with his fingertip.

"You know what I think?" he answered. "I think the job needed a bigger man than you, or me, or any of us. It would take a whale of a big man to unify Mars—all the scraps and pieces of us from Jekkara to the Pole, withdrawn into our little city-shells, sitting in the dust and hugging our memories. If we could find a Goliath like that, there might still be a chance."

"You might as well ask for Phobos to balance those bells in your ear." St. John leaned back and closed his eyes. He looked indescribably bitter and tired.

"Besides," he added, with a faint smile, "if we found a Goliath, someone else would find a David to slay him."

CHAPTER V

THERE was fresh air. There was pain. There was darkness threaded with a greenish glow. Rick stirred.

After a long time he was on his hands and knees, coughing in the dust. Back of him about three feet he was aware of a solid mass walling him in. Ahead there was a ragged rift in the blackness, through which seeped moonlight.

In the moonlight, he saw Mayo's face, still and white as stone.

He put his hand on her throat. It was warm. There was a pulse-beat. The discovery brought him happiness and relief.

He spoke to her. She moaned faintly, and that was all.

Rick crawled past her and shoved against the stuff barring his way. It was rotten, already half gone from the shaking of the slide. Presently the hole was big enough to get through.

It came to him to wonder why the worm's fossil head had not collapsed with the rest of it. There was enough moonlight coming in now to show how close they had come to dying. He looked at the upper surface, almost touching his face.

Then he understood. The worm's digging end had been sheathed with armor plate like the point of a drill, and it was still as strong as a granite arch.

Rick patted it and smiled. Then he crawled out, backward, dragging Mayo's dead weight.

He found himself high on the face of a crumbling cliff. The worm had died with its head not two feet from open water. Now there was no water. There was a lonesome, aimless wind and a maze of shadows racing under the swinging moons, and the cold dry smell of dead land.

At the foot of the cliff was a tumbled slope covered with gray-green moss, and then the desert began. It stretched as far as Rick could see, in bleached waves of sand that rolled like surf under the wind and the moon-shadows.

Out across it, far out, there was a city.

The city lay in the bed of the dry sea, thrusting its marble spires to the sky in a stricken gesture of prayer. Even while Rick watched it, it flickered like a breaking dream, obscured by drifting veils of dust.

It was the only thing in the whole landscape that held even a suggestion of human life. Rick got stiffly to his feet. His whole body ached, but he could make it work. He went down the cliff, sliding, half falling, dragging the unconscious girl. His shackle chain made a loud ringing jangle against the rock.

He got Mayo up into his arms. Her throat and arms were foam-white in the moonlight, her thick hair falling dark against Rick's skin. They were both half naked, dusty, stained with blood.

He walked out across the sand, setting one foot doggedly before the other. The swinging chain tolled in the silence like a cracked bell.

He was close to the city when little winged people appeared. Rick remembered having heard legends of them. Like the anthropoids, they were end-products, the left-overs of a race incredibly ancient, once powerful, now reduced to a mere forgotten handful clinging to empty cities lost in the sand—cities that had once been island kingdoms in a blue sea.

The winged ones drifted out from the white towers, out across the little racing moons. They were light and indescribably beautiful, and their wings shimmered with soft secret fires like opals under mist. They clustered round and followed Rick, who tramped on doggedly. They tossed on the wind like huge petals, making no sound. Rick could see their eyes, glowing with a faint phosphorescence.

Presently a marble wall loomed up in front of Rick and halted him.

He laid the girl carefully on the sand and turned around. He had no particular idea of what he was going to do. The gossamer creatures fluttered down onto the blowing sand. They were human in body, slender and graceful, wearing only short kilts. There were both men and women. Their skin was covered with a fine silky fur, almost like bird-down, and they were no more than four feet tall.

One of the men landed nearby. His handsome little face held neither friendliness nor enmity. "You are Rick," he said in a clear, soft voice. Then he whipped a pencil-tube from his girdle and fired.

Rick slid down into utter darkness. The last conscious picture he took with him was not of the man with the tube, but of a tiny woman, poised like the Winged Victory of Samothrace in the greenish moonlight, watching him with huge, still eyes.

It was the eyes most of all he remembered.

He lay on his back, comfortably, on a pile of silks and furs. He was rested and without pain, except for a slight stiffness. His hands were still chained.

The little woman sat beside him, her slender body shining like new gold in a flood of sunlight from a huge arched window high in the wall. A second glance told Rick she was little more than a girl, with all the beauty that blossoms just across the threshold from childhood. Her hand lay small and warm on Rick's bare chest.

"I have been finding out if you live," she said. "You live strongly."

Rick laughed and sat up. "What's your name?"

"Kyra."

He stirred her hand gravely. It was like a doll's hand.

Somebody near stirred and yawned.

"Your mate is awake," Kyra said. Her speech was pure High Martian, and a little difficult for Rick to follow.

43

"Mate?" He shook his head. "No. Just a swell girl I almost died with." He got up. Mayo was sitting up on a second heap of furs and bright cloths. She smiled.

"Hello, Rick. For heaven's sake where are we, and how did we get here?" She stared at Kyra.

Rick told her what he knew. "The city is called Caer Hebra," Kyra explained. "We have lived in it always, since the world was. There were many of us, once."

Rick looked around him. They were on a sort of broad terrace, inlaid magnificently with colored stones Rick had no names for. The pattern had a curious infinite quality, without beginning or end. It did strange things to anyone who looked too long. Above them, the roof soared in a pure arch of veined marble.

Only one great window could be seen. There were bas-reliefs on the walls, alive and almost breathing. They showed men and women like Kyra, only they were as big as Rick and Mayo. There were trees in the pictures, birds and beasts and once a sea with ships on it.

Rick also noticed a low, carved railing, and in the centre of it, steps. They were wide enough to march an army down, and they descended majestically into blue shadows and—sand!

It choked the vast hall below, flowing around the waists of sculptured figures, leaving here and there an impotent pleading hand or a half-smothered head where the statutory had been set lower. It crawled out from the high window, lapping at the steps.

Rick became aware of a peculiar rustling sound, like the breathing of a sleeping giant, the rubbing of the desert against the outer walls.

"There are many levels below this," said Kyra. "When my father was a child he played here, and there was no sand." She looked up at the window. A feathery plume blew in and sifted down to the terrace. Rick shivered.

He realized presently that both he and Mayo had been washed and treated with ointments. Kyra set food before them, bringing it from a table beside a massive bronze door. They ate.

"Kyra, what goes on here?" Rick said. "I remember some guy rayed me. How did he know my name?"

Kyra explained, and Rick's face hardened.

"A blood debt!" he said. "By golly, if they think they're going to sacrifice me, they're wrong!"

"My people will come at dusk to carry you back to Ruh." Kyra's luminous eyes held a shimmer of tears. "They will kill you," she whispered. "And you live—so strongly!"

She caught his hands suddenly, stretching her little self up to him. "I've heard them talk. I know the prophecy—your 'shadow over Mars.' They hate and fear you." Her next words were almost choked by tears and eagerness, and came tumbling out in an incoherent flood.

"I think you would bring life to Mars instead of death," she said. "You have life in you, so much life, and we are dying. Don't let them kill you, Rick!"

He smiled and stroked her feathery soft hair. "Better not let your people hear you talk like that. They know you're here?"

"No. Oh, Rick!"

She looked up at him. He bent and kissed her small trembling lips and suddenly she pulled away from him. For the first time she was shy. Spreading her wings, she darted away up the shaft of sunlight and was gone.

Rick sat down, rather helplessly, and looked at Mayo. There were tears in her brown eyes.

"Yeah," said Rick softly. "Isn't it!"

"Rick, I don't understand. What prophecy?"

He told about the seeress.

"I didn't mean to kill her! But she had me crazy. Also she tried to knife me." He tilted his head back so Mayo could see the half-healed cut on his throat.

She didn't say anything. She sat staring at him with such an intent and yet distant look that presently he moved restlessly.

It wasn't so much her look that disturbed him. It was because her hair was afire with sunlight and her skin was like Venusian mist at dawn, lucent pearl flushed over with sultry warmth. A muscle began to twitch in his cheek.

She rose and put her hands on his arms and studied him.

"The old woman was right," she said. "Kyra's right. There's strength in you, Rick. It's sleeping, but it's there. You've never done much with your life, have you?"

"I've enjoyed it, most of it."

"But you haven't built things. You haven't been going anywhere. Have you thought, Rick, that maybe there was something in that prophecy?"

He laughed. "I'd look fine, wouldn't I, as a shining savior!"

"I think," she said quietly, "you might look very fine."

He didn't move for a long moment, didn't breathe. Then he took her in his arms and kissed her. Presently, they drew apart.

46

"Rick, we must have a talk," she said then. "There isn't much time, and we've got to do something!"

"There's nothing to do, baby. Maybe later, there'll be a break. But right now, unless we can sprout wings like the kid, we've got to wait. Anyway, they've got nothing against you. You're in the clear."

"Don't tell me that!" Mayo stirred impatiently against the white fur on which she was lying. "Listen, Rick. Back there in that tunnel you said you wanted to drive Fallon and his gang off Mars."

Rick nodded. His cat-eyes blazed.

"Then will you come in with us, with Hugh St. John and me?" she asked him. "Rick, I tell you union is the only hope for Mars. Maybe you're the man who can bring it about. That old woman didn't talk like a hysteric, an ordinary crystal-gazer. She talked sense. That conception of a fan-shaped future is fundamental even on Earth. Many scientists accept it as sound theory."

She sat up, flushed and shaken with excitement, gripping his arm with hurtful strength.

"Take hold of your future, Rick! Mould it, build it, make it a great, towering thing that people will remember as long as they have tongues to talk about it!"

He stared at her, through her and beyond her. He began to tremble.

He rose abruptly, pacing the inlaid terrace. "My shadow," he whispered. "My shadow over Mars."

Mayo straightened slowly, watching him. An odd look came into her face—a faint, uncertain fear.

"Why not? By golly, why not!" He stopped, talking to her not as an individual but only as a point on which to focus his voice. There was a fire in him suddenly. The blaze of it spread through him until,

47

in the sunlight, he looked to her like legendary Talos, still hot from the forges.

"Why not?" he repeated. "Fallon, St. John, Storm —why not me? Take hold of my future. Sure. My future, and a world. A whole round world just waiting for somebody to pick it up. Some guy's hand will grab it. Why not mine?"

Silence, with the marble vault still echoing.

"Rick!" Mayo whispered.

He only half saw her. "You know who I am" he said, slowly. "Richard Gunn Urquhart." He pronounced it as though it had a tremendous cabalistic meaning. "I never realized that before. I guess I never really knew I was alive."

He threw back his head and laughed.

Silence, and the ringing echoes. The sunlight faded from the window. Mayo sat on the heap of furs and bright silks, unstirring.

He knelt beside her and took her in his arms.

"We'll go up together," he said. "You're the woman I need—a strong woman, to go beside me like a sword. Together, Mayo! And I'll give you Mars to wear on a chain around your neck!"

He kissed her. Her lips were cold and unresponsive, and there was a bitterness on them, a taste of tears.

He drew back, suddenly chilled. "What's the matter?"

She looked up at him. Tears welled and ran down her cheeks, shining palely in the dying light. She was not sobbing. There was an emotion within her too deep for sobs.

"I love you, Rick," she told him.

"Sure. And I love you."

"No. There's no love in you, Rick. Not the kind

48

of love I mean. Part of you has come awake—the sleeping thing the old woman saw and was afraid of —your strength. But it hasn't any soul."

His eyelids narrowed. "What are you talking about?"

"I thought you were the man we needed, just as Kyra did. A strong man, to bring life to a dying world. But you don't even know what we're talking about. You'll bring death, Rick. Death and destruction, if you live."

He released her slowly and stood up. "I don't get it. You wanted me to take Mars, didn't you?"

"I wanted you to save Mars. To build, to restore, to create."

"Have I said I wouldn't?"

"Will you?"

He tried to hold her gaze and then turned away irritably. "Bosh! Give me time! I haven't even started to think yet."

"Will you give Hugh his chance to work, as he's dreamed of working?"

He turned on her, with a look of feral ugliness.

"Listen Mayo. I've never worn anybody's collar. I'm not making any promises, or any guesses. I don't know how anything's going to shape up. But whatever I build I'll build in my own way, on my own plans." He swore furiously. "If that isn't just like a dame! For the first time I realize what a chance this offers. After a lifetime of taking the boot from the guys higher up, I see a way to maybe get a little higher than anybody else. And right away you start tying my hands, shutting gates on me!"

He went over to the rail and stood scowling at the sand below. Then he came back.

"All right, I'll be honest with you. All this is a

pretty new idea, though I guess I've been thinking about it in the back of my mind ever since the old woman said that. But I don't give a hang for Mars, or the Martians, or Hugh St. John. I care about Richard Gunn Urquhart, and it's good that I do because nobody else does or ever has. I want two things— to pay Storm and Fallon back what I owe them and to see what I can make for myself out of a world nobody else can handle. You got that?"

She nodded. "Yes, Rick. I've got it."

He watched her silently. Then he laughed.

"All this rowing, when I'll maybe be dead in a couple of days anyhow!" He dropped down beside her. "Look, Mayo. We found each other. We'll always belong to each other, because two people can't go through what we did without fusing a part of them together. But there's more than that with us. We don't know each other yet, and there's lots of ways we won't agree. But somewhere, somehow, we click, and that's the important thing. I never felt that way with anybody else. It's as though a part of me had been missing, and suddenly it just slipped into place."

He stared at her with a sort of comic wonderment. "Hey! You know you're the first dame I ever stopped to explain to? Anybody else, man or woman, until a couple of minutes ago, would have got their teeth slapped in!"

Mayo laughed suddenly, a shaken sort of laughter that ended in a sob. She put her arms around him.

"You're just a kid, Rick," she said. "You never grew up." She drew his head down. "Maybe," she whispered, "there is a soul there somewhere. Maybe it just needs love to wake it up."

50

Their lips met. And then, in the dim silence, the brazen doors crashed open.

CHAPTER VI

UP ABOVE, the little racing moons seemed close, frighteningly close against the starshot sky. The wind cut like a knife. Rick lay motionless in the cradle of broad straps and watched four pairs of wings beat the night above him, at the ends of four stout ropes.

Off to his right Mayo McCall lay in a similar cradle, carried by four more of the little men of Caer Hebra.

The Mars landscape slid by silently, far below. There were endless reaches of sand, flowing under the restless wind and the shadows, chains of mountain peaks, worn blunt by the feet of uncounted milennia, and the desolate wastes of the sea-bottoms. Here and there a marble city gleamed under the moons, like the face of a dead woman half concealed by vines and creeping verdure.

Presently, far off to one side, Rick saw the great sprawling blaze of the Terran Exploitations Company. The winged men began to drop in a long arc, and then the towers of Ruh lifted darkly into the night sky.

Jagged fingers of stone shot up as though to grasp them. Rick's heart stuck in his throat. Blurred light and shadow flickered past him, carved monsters brushed his flesh—and then, with no more than a slight jar, he was lying on a broad terrace, with Mayo not far off. Kilted warriors stood with drawn swords in the shadows. The men of Caer Hebra folded their wings and bowed with easy grace of men who give respect but not servility.

The man they bowed to was lean and sinewy, harnessed in the worn leather of a common soldier. A wolf-faced man, with eyes that caught the moonlight in points of brilliant greenish flame.

"Loose their feet," he said.

He gave Mayo one slow look that sent the blood up into her face, and then turned to Rick. He watched while the Earthman got to his feet, his chained hands clasped in front of him.

Rick waited, not speaking. His eyes had the same remote and deadly look of a captive tiger.

After a long time the lean man laughed softly and nodded.

"I am Beudach," he said, as one speaking to an equal. "My master waits."

He bowed ceremoniously to the men of Caer Hebra and motioned them to precede him. The guards closed in. Mayo moved close to Rick. Her hands were bound, but their elbows touched.

They followed Beudach into the tower. No one noticed the shadow sliding down the moonlight on silent moth-wings; a small shadow that swooped in and clung trembling to a stone gargoyle, hidden in heavy darkness.

Far below in the deserted streets of Ruh, a man walked restlessly. A huge man clad in black, whose boot-heels struck the worn stones in uneven rhythm. He walked alone. Men watched him from behind locked shutters, but no one moved to touch him. The polished butts of twin blasters glinted on his lean hips. His course was aimless, his expression strangely remote.

Quite suddenly he stopped. He raised his head slowly, turning a bit where he stood, like a hound questing.

His black eyes lifted to the towers of the King City. The light of the twin moons caught in them and burned, a phosphorescent green. Then he smiled and limped swiftly away toward the city wall. . . .

The throne room blazed with an extravagance of torches behind bronze-shuttered windows. Smoke hung in a blue haze under the carven vault. Through it faded banners and tarnished shields caught the shaking light in glints of dull crimson, purple, and gold.

Twelve men sat around the blood-red table, war chiefs from the twelve principal city-states that owed homage to Ruh. The boy-king Haral was in his high seat, and his dark, worn mother sat at his left, watching them all with bitter rage.

The hall was still when Beudach came in with guests, guards, and prisoners. But Rick, looking at their proud, sullen faces, knew that there had been trouble a moment before—high tempers, with words to match them. Jealousy was here—the scramble for precedence. They were fighting for that, before they thought of the battle of Mars.

Beudach took his post at Haral's right. The men of Caer Hebra bowed and moved to places at the table. Rick and Mayo were left alone before the high seat, the guards withdrawn somewhat behind them.

From a dense patch of shadow near Haral's feet came a quick harsh sigh, like the hiss of a coiling snake. Llaw the dwarf moved out into the torchlight, smiling.

Rick faced them all, erect and easy, his elbow

touching Mayo. His hard face was impassive. Inside, he was tense.

"You know why you are here?" Haral inquired.

"I do."

The boy-king stood up. He trembled with excitement.

"You men!" he cried. "You fighting men of Mars! Here is the Earthman of the prophecy. Through him alone can the invaders gain dominion over our world."

He flung out his hand. The gesture was theatrical. It might have been funny. It wasn't. There was a great blazing dignity in the boy. Rick nodded to himself with a reluctant admiration.

Haral's voice rang like a silver trumpet. "Look at him, you men of Mars! Tonight we stand at the crossroads. Tomorrow there will be only one highway, leading straight to victory—and freedom for Mars!"

A shout went up, and on the heels of it Parras the seer stepped out of the shadows behind the high seat.

"Lord," he said. "I must tell you this again. I have sent my mind into the future, and I have seen a third road. A black road, Lord, not far ahead. I can only say—be quick!"

Haral laughed. He was young. Very young. "We have destiny by the throat tonight, Parras!" He turned to the dwarf. "The debt is yours, Llaw. And according to the blood right, you can choose your own way to collect it. There is the Earthman. See that he pays!"

The dwarf leaped down from the dais, silently, with the deadly grace of a cat pouncing.

"Wait a minute!" said Rick.

Beudach's wolfish eyes flickered with disappointment. Haral stared at Rick in wonder. "Would you plead for your life?" Haral asked.

Rick laughed. "That would do me plenty of good wouldn't it! No." He nodded to Mayo. "It's about this girl."

Haral frowned, almost as though he hadn't noticed her before.

"I want her turned loose, not touched." Rick said. "You have nothing against her."

Beudach was not disappointed now. He was pleased.

"Lord, she is his mate," Llaw said.

Rick ignored him. "We met in a tight spot, and got out of it together. She hardly knows me." He didn't look, but he hoped she wasn't blushing.

"It's not important now," Haral gestured. "Llaw!"

Rick opened his mouth angrily. Llaw gestured. The guards moved in. Rick shut his teeth together, leaving them bare, and shoved Mayo carefully out of the way.

He put three men down with his shackle chain and two more with his feet before somebody slammed the flat of a sword blade down across his temple. He felt two more blows before the darkness closed in. Through the last of the light he saw Beudach's face, set in an expression of disgust. Beudach was looking at Llaw. . . .

When Rick again regained consciousness, there were jagged streaks of crimson across the black. They came with a strangely regular beat. Somewhere far off a woman was screaming. It was not a fear-scream, or hysteria. It was the angry shriek of a clawed animal.

Rick opened his eyes.

Red waving curtains hid the throne room. There was movement beyond them, distant and unreal. The shrieking came from beyond the curtains, and a swinging clash of hammers on metal that seemed very close.

Presently he realized that the redness was pain, pain so intense that almost he could see it.

It seemed to him that he was high up, very high, looking down upon the crimson, hazy sea.

The screaming stopped.

There was darkness again for a period of time. When it lifted he could hear only a sort of uneasy mutter. The pain had shifted for his mind had slipped free into dimensions where it was aware of the pain but was disconnected from it. He opened his eyes again.

His head was hanging forward. He saw his own body, erect, stripped naked, shining with sweat like polished bronze, streaked with blood. His feet rested on a transverse ornamental beam of some dark blue wood, cracked and darkened by age. The hilts of two heavy daggers stood up through his arches. The daggers were bright in the torchlight. Very bright.

Far below him was the stone floor.

Slowly he turned his head. It was heavy and took a long time to turn. He saw his left arm stretched out against the wall. The fingers of his hand were curled laxly around the hilt of a third dagger, driven through his palm into a crack between two blocks of stone.

He knew without looking that it was the same on his right. He let his head drop forward again.

Mayo knelt on the stones. Her face was turned up to him. He smiled.

Llaw the dwarf crouched, hugging his knees, almost in the attitude of a man worshipping. He was alone. His gaze fixed on Rick, unwinking, burning with a deep, insane light.

Back further, the twelve war-chiefs and the men

of Caer Hebra sat at the blood-red table, drinking, talking low in a desultory way. They avoided each other's eyes and did not look up. Haral slumped in the high seat, staring at the rug of virgin's hair. His face was white, sick. Beside him the Queen-Mother sat unmoved, watching the man on the wall. To her he was not human, not worthy of the sympathy she would have given to a beast. He was an Earthman.

Beudach rose suddenly from the dais. His face held a cold fury and his hand twitched over his dagger hilt.

"By the gods of my people!" he snarled explosively. "Isn't this enough?"

Llaw smiled faintly. He didn't move. Parras spoke out of the shadows.

"Lord, I beg you," he said. "Finish this!"

Haral raised his head, carefully not looking at Rick. "Llaw?"

"By the blood right, Majesty," said Llaw softly. "This is my choice."

Haral fell back in his high seat.

Beudach stared upward. His eyes met Rick's dark amber gaze, and gradually a silence came over the hall so that the slow splashing of blood-drops onto the stone floor was clearly audible.

"I am ashamed," said Beudach. "For my people I am ashamed."

He turned and suddenly, moved forward, set his foot under Llaw's chin and threw him flat. Then he drew his dagger.

"Blood right or not, Earthman, you deserve a man's death!" he cried. His hands swept back for the throw.

Llaw yowled like a mad cat and flung himself at Beudach, incredibly swift. Beudach staggered.

The knife whirled, glittering, through the torchlight, struck wide, and dropped clanging onto the stones. Beudach snarled and got his hands around Llaw's throat.

Suddenly, out in the vaulted halls beyond the bronze doors of the throne room, a man screamed. And as though that sound were the trigger, a perfect fury of noise burst out.

Every man in the throne room came to his feet. No one spoke. Blades flashed out of scabbards. Beudach raised his head, and between his wide-spread feet the heels of the dwarf drummed a diminishing tattoo and were silent.

Beudach dropped the body. He didn't look at it. He went to Haral, drawing the sword that hung behind his shoulder.

Mayo was standing now, pressed against the wall. By stretching her bound hands high she could reach Rick's feet, but not the dagger hilts. She looked up into his face. She tried to speak, but nothing would come. His sweat and blood dropped onto her white skin, shining in the red glare.

Rick's lips formed the words, "I love you." He smiled. And then the bronze doors crashed open and Jaffa Storm was standing there, with his Venusians and the black anthropoids crowding in behind him.

CHAPTER VII

FULLY conscious, Rick watched from the high wall. His mind was clear, detached, perfectly sane. But in his eyes, in his face, something had changed. It was like the chilling and tempering of the weapon from the soft hot steel. Never again would he be careless and happy-go-lucky.

He watched the Martians fight and go down under the blasters of Storm's men. Guards came. The hall was choked with warriors. The huge white-haired Venusians, the blasters, and the black apes cut them down.

From outside, in the halls and the streets beyond, from over the whole city, rose an animal howl, mingled with the thunder of fighting and the saw-edged whine of Banning shockers.

In the throne room, one by one, the torches were trampled out.

After a time there was silence. In the darkness of tattered flags and forgotten glories, one torch still burned in a high sconce, spilling a red and shaken light over the man pinned by knives against the stone wall. The Venusians and the apes withdrew, taking their dead. Outside fighting still continued, but the sound of it was distant, muffled. Mayo had not moved from the place where she pressed close against the wall, touching Rick's feet.

Jaffa Storm came and stood before them.

He looked upward for a long while without speaking. Then he smiled and stretched his giant body, muscle by muscle, as a panther does. His black eyes held a deep pleasure.

" 'The wind is rising,' " he quoted softly. "Bah! it's blown itself out! These men were the leaders of Mars. What's left—a few barbarians and the Thinkers at the Pole—are nothing." He laughed quietly. "I knew they were here. I knew you were here. I have as much knowledge as their seers. Perhaps more."

Mayo had slid silently to her knees, her bound hands on the shadowy floor.

Storm studied Rick. "There was some prophecy, wasn't there? And a blood debt." He nodded. "You've caused me a lot of trouble, Rick. That stone hurt. You made me look foolish when you got away, and you inspired a lot more men to try it. Besides, there was something—else."

Rick laughed, a harsh whisper of sound. "That's true. I saw you take the boot from a girl."

Storm nodded. He leaned over and caught Mayo by the shoulder.

She came up fast. She had Beudach's knife in her hands. Storm let his breath out, hard. There was a blur of motion and sound. The dagger rang on the stones and Mayo was lifted in Storm's arms.

"You're a strong man, Rick. You'll live for quite a while. I don't think anyone will come here just yet —there's no one left in the King City, and they're still busy down below—and if anyone does, I don't think they'll take you down."

"Such an idea pleases you, doesn't it," sneered Rick.

Again Storm laughed. "It does," he said. "You were to rule Mars, weren't you, according to the prophecy? They cling to the belief of the fan-shaped future, the infinite roads. Somewhere, Rick, you took the wrong turning!"

He went away. Rick watched the warm sheen of torchlight in Mayo's hair as far as he could see it, and then listened to the limping tread of Storm's boots fading down the hall.

He was alone.

He tried, once, to see if he could move the blades

that pinned him. After that he hung motionless, breathing in deep, harsh sighs.

Presently, somewhere in the dimness, something stirred.

It was Beudach, dragging himself from under a heap of bodies by the high seat. He crawled among them on his hands and knees, searching the faces. Save for his labored breathing, he made no sound, not even when he found what he sought.

In the guttering torchlight, Rick saw the ivory gleam of Haral's body as Beudach raised it in his arms. Rising slowly to his feet Beudach walked, erect and without swaying, to the dais and laid the boy in the high seat, his dark head propped against the carved back, his hands along the arm rests. The red light caught in his open eyes, and on the worn bosses of his collar.

Beudach found a sword and laid it across Haral's knees. Then he sank down on the dais.

After a while he raised his head and looked at Rick. There was a light of prophecy in his eyes.

"You will not die," he panted, solemnly.

In a whisper, fully as hoarse, the man on the wall answered, "No."

"You will rule Mars."

"I—will—rule—Mars!"

Silence. Presently Beudach nodded. "For good or ill, the road is taken. And you're a man."

"Beudach," Rick said.

"Yes?"

"With my own hands, Beudach—my own hands!"

Beudach looked from Rick to the dead boy and back again. He smiled. Then he let himself down from the dais and began to crawl slowly and painfully across the floor toward Rick.

Suddenly he stopped.

"Someone's coming," he muttered.

Out in the darkness of the corridor there was a soft rustle of movement, and then a faint scream—shocked and strangled.

"Rick! Rick!"

The quick silken rustle of wings in the dusk, and then Kyra was clinging to the carved stones beside Rick, her great eyes wide, stunned, and tearless.

"I followed them, Rick," she whimpered. "I thought maybe there'd be something, something I could do to help you. Oh, Rick."

He smiled at her. "You can, baby." His speech was slow and thick. "You can pull out these knives."

Her tiny face whitened, but she nodded. From the floor Beudach spoke.

"Wait. He'll fall. The ladders are still here. Help me."

She fluttered down. Between them they raised one of the light metal ladders that had been used to get Rick up there.

Very, very slowly Beudach climbed it and pulled the daggers from the Earthman's feet.

After that, Rick was only partly conscious when they pulled the blades from his hands. He knew that Kyra's wings beat rapidly as she held him up. He sensed Beudach's wiry, dogged strength. He tried to help them, but there was a coldness on him, and a roaring in his ears.

Presently there was a hot sting of wine in his throat. He lay propped against the wall at the foot of the ladder. Beudach crouched beside him, with a goblet. Shaking with exhaustion, Kyra was binding strips of cloth around his hands and feet.

Beudach dropped the goblet. There was a cold

sweat on his face. He raised something from the floor beside him.

The iron Collar of Ruh.

"Listen, Earthman. Our time is finished. Whatever time is to be on Mars will be new, and different. And it will be your time."

He stopped to fight for breath.

"This collar is the symbol of kingship over half of Mars. Where Ruh and the Collar lead, Mars follows. I'm going to put it on your neck. There's a hidden blade in the lock. Only one or two men in each generation know the secret, and when anyone else tampers with it he gets death from the poison on that blade, and the lock stays locked. The collar will be your key to the loyalty of the Martians. What you do with that loyalty will bring your own destiny upon you."

He stopped again.

"Why do you give me the collar?" Rick whispered.

"Because that's the way the road leads. Because you will destroy the Company, and the men of the Company. Because there is no Martian left with strength to wear the Collar—now. Things may not be that way always, but the future will have to take care of its own."

He placed the iron collar around Rick's throat. It was still faintly warm from Haral's young flesh.

Beudach looked a long time into Rick's cold, fathomless yellow eyes. Once his hand moved, almost as though to take the collar back. Then he closed the lock.

"There's a secret passage leading to safety out of this place," Beudach went on. "Press the sixteenth boss to the left of the main hall, up, then down. More than one lord of Ruh has gone that way to safety. And hurry." He looked once more at Rick. "Remember, Earthman—that collar won't save your life if you betray it."

Rick's eyes held no emotion.

Kyra came back. She took hold of Rick, half dragging, half carrying him to a narrow black rectangle in the wall.

Beudach sighed. Slowly, as though he were settling down to sleep, he fell sideways and lay still, with his head on Haral's feet.

Then came a grating sound as Kyra sealed the secret passage with a block of stone, and cold dry black closed around Rick. . . .

Many hours later, in the glassite-walled office on the top floor of the Company's Administration pylon, Jaffa Storm was sprawled lazily on a couch, smoking. He did not appear to be paying much attention to Ed Fallon.

Fallon was moving with short angry strides up and down in front of the desk. His blocky face was ugly.

"Blast it all!" he burst out finally. "To pull a stunt like that over some dame was reckless folly. Do you know how many men you got killed?"

Storm shrugged. "They were Venusians. They like to die fighting. I've got more coming."

"Sure, that's easy. But what about the Martians you left dead all over the streets? You fool! Don't you realize it may get us kicked straight off the planet?"

Storm's eyebrows went up derisively. "Who'll do the kicking?"

"The Martian Planetary Government will complain to Earth, and the Interplanetary Coordination Authority!"

"You don't say?" Storm sat up. His black eyes were remote and faintly contemptuous. "I've already lodged a complaint with the MPG. It won't go any further."

Fallon stood still. His eyes grew narrow.

"They had two Earthlings prisoner, didn't they?" Storm went on. "One a woman, and both employees of the Company. They pinned the man up on the wall with knives, didn't they? The devil only knows what they were going to do with the woman. All right. We had to rescue them, didn't we? And where could we go for legal protection? Besides, we have evidence the Marshies were getting ready for a massacre. The Planetary Government doesn't want trouble, Fallon. They've got nothing to back up their trouble with."

He laughed. "Along with the complaint I sent a big fat check to be used on one of their restoration schemes!"

Fallon smiled, without humor. "Clever kid. And what about Ruh? What about all the Marshies this side of Kahora? How are they going to feel about you blasting their king and their top men to Kingdom Come?"

"They can feel any way they want to," said Storm evenly. "I've got blasters. I've got a ring of Bannings around the walls, and plenty of Venusians, with more coming. There's no law on Mars but strength—and I've got that, too."

There was a new and insolent note in Storm's voice which worried Fallon. He turned back to the desk and sat down.

"All right, Storm," he said. "Maybe you're so smart you can get away with it."

"You bet I can get away with it. Listen, Fallon!

Those men in the throne room were plotting to get your scalp. We'd have to fight them sooner or later. I preferred it sooner."

"You preferred it. Yeah. You use my men and equipment, you risk my company and everything I've put into this dustball of a planet, just because you had a personal grudge to satisfy. And all of it without saying a word to me. Maybe you think you'd be better off running this show."

Storm's gaze slid speculatively over Fallon.

"You've got it so it practically runs itself." He leaned over and crushed out his cigarette. He went on casually, "You're getting flabby, Ed. Physically, I mean. You're turning into the typical tycoon, the guy who sits behind the desk and grows a veranda, and only gets a kick out of doing tricks with his brain. I've watched you, when I've had to take some of these tough boys to the wall. You don't like it, Ed. It makes you sick. What happened in Ruh made you sick, and you were so scared you almost passed out. You're getting old, Ed, beginning to slow down and get cautious. I've put over the first blow, but there'll be other blows. Other companies, hijacking, throat-cutting, all the rest of it. Mars isn't a world you can afford to get old on, Ed."

Fallon sucked his breath in, softly. "You're a liar, Jaffa."

"Take it any way you want," retorted Storm.

"I'll take it the way you mean it. You want the Company for yourself."

"The Company means Mars, Ed. I want Mars."

Fallon nodded. He did not seem particularly surprised. He let his red head drop forward, crumpling slightly upon himself where he sat.

His movement, when it came, was very quick. Jaffa

Storm was a little quicker. The blaster echoes faded quickly into the soundproofing. There was a seared spot on a pillar next to Storm's head. Fallon still sat behind the desk. He had now neither a face nor any further interest in the future of his Company.

Storm rose and limped over to the telescreen. He called Vargo and gave instructions. Then he went out, fastening the door behind him.

A few moments later he let himself into a locked apartment in another part of the compound.

Mayo McCall rose from the couch where she had been lying and stood back against the wall. She did not tremble or cry or become hysterical. She said nothing. There was something deadly in her brown eyes.

Storm smiled and sat down. He admired her frankly. Her clothing had been brought to her from her old quarters. In place of the ragged coverall, she was wearing a simple draped tunic of dull bronze cloth that made her hair look like fire. The cut of the garment emphasized the supple magnificence of body that the coverall had only hinted at.

"I've taken over the Company," Storm said quietly.

Her brows rose slightly. She watched him, speechlessly.

"Don't you want to know what I'm going to do with you?" asked Storm.

"Does it matter?"

"Maybe. Because I'm not going to do anything."

She stared at him.

"Well, perhaps I should say anything—for a while." He studied her for a long moment, half smiling. "You made me an offer once, Mayo."

She laughed. "Don't tell me it's still open!"

"It could be." He leaned forward. "Listen, Mayo.

67

I own the Company, and the Company will own Mars. This is a fallow world. The ploughing of it will grow a crop of wealth and power that hasn't been known since the development of the frontier continents centuries ago on Earth—and wasn't known then, really, because they were only playing with pieces of a world."

His black eyes held a deep, smoldering heat.

"I've never seen a woman like you, Mayo. I don't know what it is. I've seen plenty of them with as much looks, maybe more. But you've got something different, something that's you. And I want it. I want it so much that I'm not going to pay off what I owe you—unless you make me. Those are the cards, Mayo. Play 'em any way you want to."

He stood up. "I've got plenty of time. I don't mind waiting. In fact, I rather like it. Just remember that I'll get what I want, one way or the other, in the end."

CHAPTER VII

QUIETLY Rick lay on a shelf-bunk covered with silks and skins. There was a small window above him. Greenish moonlight fell through it, giving shape to the tiny cell-like room. It was, ironically, almost identical wth the room in which Rick had met the seeress and her blood-thirsty grandson—and the prophecy. It was hollowed in the thickness of the City Wall, and from above or far below on the dead sea-bottom the window would show merely as an irregularity in the stones.

There was one door, leading into the passage that came under the streets of Ruh from the throne room. The passage branched here. Kyra, exploring cautiously, had found that it led through a balanced stone into a back street of the Thieves' Quarter.

The little hideout had been thoughtfully provisioned, evidently as a traditional duty rooted in more turbulent days of the city's history. There was clothing, food, wine, weapons, and everything necessary to the care of wounds.

Rick held his hands up in the shaft of moonlight and flexed the fingers. Already, in the four days he had been here, the wounds had begun to heal well. It was the same with his feet. The daggers, fortunately, had been razor sharp and had slid through between bone and tendon with a minimum of damage.

Rick smiled faintly. He dozed again. He had been sleeping a great deal. His body, naturally strong and toughened by the hard life he had led, was almost normal again.

Presently there was a flutter of wings outside, and Kyra pulled her tiny, little self through the window.

Rick woke immediately. "Did you find her?"

"Yes! Oh, Rick, she was so happy to learn you are safe. She said that only to know that was enough."

"How was she? Has Storm bothered her?"

"She's in no danger, right now," Kyra explained. "I gave her the knife. She tells you not to worry, to be careful, and—and she sends you—this!"

She placed her soft little lips against Rick's. Then, quite suddenly, she was crying, curled against his chest. He stroked her.

"You're tired," he said. "You've done too much

for me, and I've put you in too much danger. You've got to go home."

Her wings rustled sharply. "Oh, no! Rick, you need me!"

"Not that much. You saved my life, kid. Now go home, where you'll be safe."

"Rick, I can't go home! They—I don't know what they'd do to me. Besides, there isn't anything there I want, any more."

He tilted her head back. The moonlight gleamed on her young face, the slender curve of her throat.

"You know what you're saying, Kyra?" he asked her.

"I know."

"And you know what I have to say back to you."

"I know." Kyra nodded her pretty head.

"It isn't any use to tell you that this isn't love the way you think it is, and that you'll get over it."

"I won't go home, Rick. You can't make me. You can make me fly away a little but I'll come back." She spread her wings and stood up. The moonlight made her delicate fur glisten like hot silver and touched a dim opaline fire from her wings.

"I love you, Rick, but it's more than that. I love Mars. You're going to make Mars a world where people can hope, and look forward. You don't know what it is, Rick, to be young in a dead city, with nowhere to look but back! And I want a part in the building. Even if it's just a little tiny part, to know that I've helped will be enough. You can't take that away from me."

He looked at her for a long moment, without speaking. A strange, stony look hardened his face briefly. An expression almost of cruelty came into his eyes as he squared his jaw. Then he shrugged.

"No, I don't suppose I can, short of killing you," he said quietly. "All right, Kyra. We'll play it that way."

She dropped cross-legged by the low bunk, smiling, triumphant.

"Anybody around the Company see you?" Rick went on.

"No. Not any of the times I've been there."

"Learn anything more about Storm, or the defences of the place?"

"No more than I've told you. Rick, I don't think anybody would live through an attack! On our side, I mean."

"Probably not. How does Ruh look, Kyra?"

"I saw torchlight in the streets when I came back. I think there will be trouble, very soon. Oh, Rick— there was one thing I overheard while I was hiding on a roof tonight. Storm has raided the New Town twice for men, already. The pits are working on a triple shift. Men have died."

Rick nodded. "Storm's not wasting any time." He sat up, swinging his feet over the side. "Get the bandages, baby, and tie these up, tight."

She started to protest, and then went obediently to work.

"I can't wait any longer," Rick said, half to himself. "Once they start it'll be too late, for all of us!"

The balanced stone moved silently, a few minutes later, and they stepped out warily into a narrow rat-run, hugging the foot of the Wall. It was densely shadowed, deserted except for varied smells. From somewhere ahead came a low, confused, but angry murmur.

Kyra darted off into the air and came back presently to say that there was a mob gathered in the

Thieves' Market, with more people coming steadily from the better Quarters of the city.

She caught Rick's arm. "They'll kill you," she whispered. "They'll tear you to pieces."

Rick smiled. It was a strange smile, without humor or humanness.

"Go on," he said. "Lead the way."

Kyra turned obediently, but her wings trailed on the dirty stones.

They went along narrow, twisting streets between buildings so ancient that the dust of their erosion lay heaped in the sheltered corners. There was nothing human in sight, nothing but rags of washing hung bannerwise from the black windows to show that people lived there at all. But Rick could sense them, in the reeking air of the place. People among whom evil was as commonplace as breathing. Phobos had set in the east, but Diemos hung low over Ruh, so low that the towers of the King City seemed to have impaled it.

The crowd roar grew steadily louder.

There was an odd quality in it. There was fury, but it was the fury of a dirge rather than a war cry.

They came to the end of the street. The mob roar, the mob smell beat back at them. The tossing glare of torches blotted out the moon. They looked into a broad square, jammed solidly with people. The leaning, settling houses shouldered up around it, and here, too, were people—hanging out of windows, clinging like swarming bees to every balcony and overhang that would give them footing.

The noise burst suddenly into a great shout, and then tapered off to silence. The voice of one man rang out, thin and bitter like a trumpet call across the field of a lost battle.

Rick began to work his way forward. No one bothered to look at him.

The man stood on a scaffold in the center of the square—the gibbet where the thieves of the Quarter meted out their own justice. He was small and wiry and grizzled, dressed in the rags of a gold-mesh tunic. His face was twisted, lined with scars, his eyes a slanted reddish topaz that burned like the torch flames.

"You know why you're here," he was shrieking. "You know what has been done. You know the men who would have freed us are dead, and our young king with them."

He paused, to let the sombre snarling response of the crowd die down.

"You know," he said quietly, "what there is left for us to do."

The yell that answered him was a pure blood-cry.

"You know they have the weapons, the walls, and the strength. All right! But they can't stop us. We won't come back—we know that, too—but before we die we'll wipe the Earthman's Company from the face of Mars!"

In the instant of silence before the shout, Rick raised his voice.

"Wait!" he bellowed.

An angry mutter spread across the square. The little man looked down at Rick. His eyes dilated. His breath sucked in harshly, and suddenly he flung his hands out to silence the crowd.

The quiet spread out from his urgent hands, crawling across the upturned faces, lapping the walls like still water, until the snapping silken rustle of the torches sounded plainly.

Rick began to climb the steps onto the scaffold.

He went slowly, but erect and without limping. He wore a purple cloak that swept from his big shoulders to his heels, held at the breast with the symbol of the Twin Moons in burning emerald.

He walked onto the platform, under the swinging chains of the gibbet. He raised his bandaged hands to the clasp and let the cloak slip down.

No one voiced a single word. Only a breath, one huge indrawn sigh, swept from wall to wall and was silent.

Rick stood perfectly still. His supple, thick-muscled body was half bared in the plain leather harness of a soldier, and around his throat, dull and battered and worn with centuries, the Collar of Ruh gave back an iron gleam to the torches.

The thief in the golden tunic goggled at him. "Who are you?" he asked.

Rick didn't raise his voice, but it rolled back off the walls.

"Richard Gunn Urquhart, the leader of the prophecy."

A sort of moan rose out of the crowd, a beast cry before blood. The thief flung his arms out.

"Wait! Wait, you people!" He stepped close to Rick, his fingers curled hungrily on his dagger hilt. "How did you, an Earthman, get the Collar of Ruh!"

"Beudach himself took it from Haral's neck after the massacre and put it on mine. You know the story of the lock. You know I'm telling the truth."

"Beudach!" whispered the thief. The name ran eerily across the square, half voiced—Beudach . . . Beudach!

"An Earthman," said the chief. "An Earthman, with the Collar of Ruh!"

He drew his knife.

Rick's face was impassive. He didn't look at the knife. He stared out over the crowd with a steady gaze.

"Listen, you people," he said. "When Beudach locked the Collar on me, he said, 'For good or ill, the road is taken.' And it is. This, out of all the roads Mars might have walked, is the one that came topmost on the wheel. You can't change that. Nobody can change it. They tried to. They pinned me to the throne-room wall with knives, but they couldn't change it."

His voice had a queer ring in it. Not fierce, or threatening, or pleading, but as though he were so completely confident that he had stopped thinking about it, and was only rehashing what they must already know.

"I'm not an Earthman. I was born in deep space, and the Jekkara Port was the first ground I ever set foot on. I belong to no world, and no race. I belong to myself, to give my loyalty where I will."

He waited, and then went on.

"Mars isn't lost, unless you go ahead and lose it," he said. "You will, if you tackle the Company this way. Kyra! Kyra, come here and tell them what you saw."

The sea of faces turned to watch her as she rose out of the dark street and came fluttering down beside Rick on the scaffold. She touched him, timidly, afraid of the crowd. Rick put his hand on her gently. Then he faced the crowd again.

"The Earthman of the Company left me hanging on those knives, to die," he shouted. "It was Kyra who saved me—she and Beudach. I owe my life to Mars."

He smiled down at Kyra.

75

"Tell them, baby," he whispered.

She told them. "You would die," she finished, "and never touch them."

An uncertain mutter of talk ran across the square. The thief leaned forward. His knife was still raised, but he seemed to have forgotten about it. His topaz eyes held a curious, unwilling respect.

"You," he said. "How would you do it?"

"If I tell you that, Jaffa Storm will know it almost as soon as you do. He has powers as great as your seers—stone walls don't stop his mind. How else do you think he knew your leaders were here ready to be killed? If he hadn't been so busy, and felt so safe, he'd have been back to spy on Ruh before this."

"Then we would just have to trust you," the thief said softly. He began to balance the dagger idly in his hand. "Beudach was a dying man."

"Tell them, Kyra," Rick said.

She stretched herself in the torch-flare, her wings spread wide.

"Listen, you Martians," she cried out furiously, "Jaffa Storm put chains on Rick and tried to make him be a slave in the mines. When Rick wouldn't submit, Storm tried to kill him. Four nights ago he left Rick hanging on the wall to die, and he took Rick's mate back with him to the Company. What more reason could a man have to want revenge?"

There was a sort of light shining out of her. Her soft young voice carried like a flute.

"Rick will lead Mars to greatness," she told them. "He will bring life back to the dying. He will give you unity, and strength."

For a long time there was silence. Then the shout came—a crashing thunder of salute that shook the stones.

Rick turned to the thief in the golden rags.

"Keep them ready," said Rick. "It won't be long. I'll send word back by Kyra when to strike."

The thief nodded. Rick held up his hands to the crowd. He smiled, but his eyes remained cold and remote, untouched. Then just as silently and as mysteriously as they had appeared, Rick and Kyra departed. . . .

Out across the sea-bottom, in the office that had been Fallon's in the Company Administration pylon, Jaffa Storm was busy—busier than Rick dreamed. He was not doing anything physically. He was sitting perfectly still, elbows on knees, his eyes closed, and his knuckles pressed in a certain curious way against his temples. He had been in contact with Rick's mind before. Now that he had the wave-length, so to speak, it was much easier to tune in. He laughed softly when Rick made his statement about Storm's mental powers and the danger of telling the battle plan.

Storm did not move until Rick was through speaking—until he had examined the unspoken things inside the Earthman's head. Then he rose, stretching, and nodded.

"A good plan," he said. "Very shrewd. It has even a fair chance of succeeding. Opposing brute force against brute force is always a gamble . . . Let's see."

He flicked on a light under a sort of table of thick frosted glass, and spun a selector dial. Presently a three-dimensional full-color miniature of the Polar area—a glorified relief map—took shape on the screen.

Jaffa Storm sat down again, taking the same posi-

tion. He stared at the screen, but his eyes were looking into some other place, much farther away.

CHAPTER VIII

HUGH ST. JOHN sighed, stretched out in a long chair,
and closed his eyes.

"Well, that's that," he said to Eran Mak. "The last
shot in my locker, the last credit in my bank account. I'm finished."

Eran Mak said nothing. He was sitting on the balcony rail, smoking, watching the easy life of Kahora
under the sunlighted dome. His swarthy piratical face
was shadowed and sombre.

"I hoped maybe you, as a Martian, would have
better luck," St. John said dully. "But they didn't let
you any farther than they did me."

The bells in Eran Mak's ear chimed as he shook
his head.

"Well, there goes Mars. Mak, just who and what
the devil are these Thinkers, that they're too blamed
good to see anybody?"

"Nobody knows, really, except that they're the
First Race, supposedly the original Martians, which
would imply that the rest of us came from somewhere
else," Mak answered. "Or else they're non-human and
preceded us in evolution. I suspect they're just a
bunch of smart people who liked to live in peace and
comfort, and so withdrew themselves behind a wall
of legend, glamour, and fear."

St. John found the strength to smile at that. "What

I love about you, Mak, is your simple faith in everything. But these Thinkers have done a lot of good from time to time."

Mak nodded. "Sure. Theoretically at least they guide the viewpoint of Mars—when they feel like bothering. It has to be some big important split, like the inter-hemispheric war back in Sixty-two Thousand and Seven, when the Sea Kings had trouble."

"Wouldn't you think this was important?" inquired St. John.

"I suppose," said Eran Mak quietly, "the Thinkers have aged with the rest of us."

There was a long silence. The city whispered below. Warm sunlight fell through the high dome, bringing a soft jewel lustre to the buildings of colored plastic, a delicate shimmer to the web of walks and roadways arching between them. The air was soft, neither warm nor cool, pleasantly scented.

Eran Mak swore with a deadly calmness and got up, sending a shower of music from the bells.

"I'm going back to Jekkara, Hugh!" he growled. "I want to breathe air again, and wear something that doesn't make people look twice to see if I'm male or female. Want to come down with me?"

"Yes, thanks, I may as well." St. John looked up and laughed, rather sheepishly. "I don't know why Mars should mean anything to me. But this is like giving up hope for a friend."

He looked down at the plastic pavement. "If I only knew what happened to Mayo."

Mak put a hand on his shoulder. St. John rose and followed him inside, to start packing.

The telescreen hummed.

"The devil with it," said St. John. He went on into the bedroom. The buzzer continued to hum stridently. Presently the tempo changed to the short insistent "urgent" signal.

St. John swore and hit the switch. The screen flickered and cleared, showing the interior of a crude public booth, liberally scrawled, carved, and initialed. The man in the booth was a stranger, big and tawny and yellow-eyed, dressed in the usual gaudy silk shirt and tight pants of a space-hand on earth-leave. His hands were bandaged.

He was not a usual space-hand. St. John suppressed a shiver of excitement.

"Hugh St. John, here," he said.

"Urquhart," answered the man. "Richard Gunn Urquhart." He pulled the bright shirt open at his throat. "You know what that is?"

Eran Mak, standing behind St. John, let his breath out in a startled curse.

"By the planets! The Collar of Ruh!"

Rick nodded. "For Mars. A united Mars. Mayo says that's what you're after."

"Mayo!" St. John gripped the edges of the screen. "Where is she? Is she all right?"

"Jaffa Storm's got her, but she's not been harmed. It's a long story, and I'll tell you later. Right now I want to know something. Do you want union enough to risk your neck for it?"

St. John drew a long breath. His eyes met Mak's briefly. "Go on," he said. "I'm listening."

"All right." Rick sketched in the details of the massacre at Ruh. "The Marshies are all set to go. The men of the New Town will be, too, when I get through with 'em. Storm has been crimping here already, and the people don't like it. But frontal attack won't be enough. Somebody's got to help us from the inside. If we can get Storm, the rest will be easy."

St. John frowned in a worried manner. "What about Fallon?"

"Storm killed him four days ago. Nobody but Storm and Mayo know about that, and probably the Venusian, Vargo. Do you think you can work it with Storm to get permission to land on the Company's 'copter deck?"

St. John frowned. "I don't know whether Storm has definitely connected Mayo with us or not, but I think he was always suspicious of me. I'll be honest with you. He'll probably let us land, all right, and then he'll blow us to Kingdom Come."

"You willing to try it?"

"Mayo's there—you're sure of that."

"I'm sure. I'll tell you about that, too."

"All right." St. John leaned closer. "There's just one thing. Who the dickens are you, and what do you want out of this?"

Rick held up his bandaged hands. "To get these around Jaffa Storm's throat."

The bells in Eran Mak's ear rang faintly. "I know you. You're Rick, the man Storm was trying to kill, the man who helped Mayo to get away, down there in the mines."

Rick stared past St. John at Eran Mak. "Well."

Mak's hot golden eyes dwelt on the iron Collar. "I'm a Jekkara man myself. But if Beudach of Ruh put that on you himself, it means plenty." He shrugged, smiling. "What have we got to lose, Hugh?"

St. John's hands trembled slightly on the edges of the screen. He was still studying Rick, with an odd intentness.

"Not a thing," he said softly. "Not a blamed thing.

All right, Rick. I'll fix it with Storm somehow. Then what?"

"Then fly down to the New Town. I'll be waiting, with everything set to go. And make it fast, St. John! Fast, before anything gets to Storm."

In the meantime, Jaffa Storm had finished his mental exploration—an effort that left him exhausted, despite his physical strength. He, of all the creatures on Mars, human, semi-human and sub-human, had seen beyond the veil of mystery that hid the Polar Cities and the Thinkers who dwelt in them.

Jaffa Storm was pleased with what he saw with his mind's eye. He gave instructions and took off northward in a one-man flier. He returned less than a full day later, tired, exultant, and bearing in his arms something wrapped in a curious shining cloth—a something that, for all its small size, bent Storm's knees with its weight. . . .

After finishing his talk with Hugh St. John, Rick walked down the main street of the New Town. It was night again. He had waited purposely until the life of the place was going full strength.

Ochre dust rose in clouds from Rick's boots. The unpaved streets, marked out at random by lines of shacks and lean-tos, were crowded with men—spacehands, placer miners, homesteaders, drifters, bums, thieves, con men—and women to match. They were predominantly from Earth, but Venus, the Asteroids, and every planetary colony was represented.

Most of the buildings on the main street were saloons and crude copies of expensive amusement places. Dream Palaces, joints dealing in exotic drugs at cut-rate prices, a couple of three-dimensional cinemas showing films several years old, and numerous girl shows featuring, "The Exotic Beauty of a Hundred Worlds—No Minors Allowed." The noise was terrific.

Rick steered around a developing brawl in mid-street and stopped in the comparative shelter of an archway. He watched for a while. There was tension about the crowd. An ugliness that had, as yet, no direction to it. Every man was armed, most of them with blasters.

He glanced up at the sky, measuring the distance between the two moons. He nodded and went on. Presently he turned into the swinging red plastic doors of "The Furnace—Hottest Spot on Mars." And the biggest spot in the New Town of Ruh.

A bunch of tired-looking Venusian girls were putting their polished-emerald bodies mechanically through a routine Rick had seen five years ago in Losanglis, back on Earth. Hard-looking men, in various stages of drunkenness, leaned on the ringside tables and carried on loud one-sided conversations with them. The long bar, backed up by an interplanetary array of liquors, mostly, and a cheap Florent mirror—the type that is sensitive only to the infrared heat rays given off by living bodies, transforming them into visible reflections with interesting results—was jammed from end to end.

Rick elbowed his way in. He ordered thil, a potent cold-green liquid from the Jekkara Low-Canals, and sipped it, studying the mirror.

Suddenly somebody down the line let out a bellow.

"Rick! Rick Urquhart!"

The volume of other noise lessened a bit, for others nearby had been startled by the tone, and the next words rang clearly.

"My stars! I thought you was dead in the Company pits!"

At the word "Company," a brassy silence descended upon the Furnace.

Rick scanned the mirror. He saw a gangling, sinewy shape gesticulating frantically at his reflection. "Texas!" he yelled, and pulled himself up on the bar.

He was aware that he had the attention of everyone in the place, including the tired chorus girls.

He walked down the bar, past rows of mugs and glasses, reached over and pulled "Texas" up beside them. They pounded each other. Texas had a tough, good-natured face with the bones sticking through his leathery skin, bad teeth, high-heeled boots, and a liquor breath that could stand by itself. He had herded meat-animals on three planets and an asteroid, and was the closest thing to a friend Rick had found in his wanderings.

"For Pete's sake, yuh old sheepherder!" yelled Texas. "I thought the crimpers got yuh, last time we was over in the Old Town."

"They did," answered Rick. "But I started a small riot in the mine and was lucky enough to get away." Rick's voice carried quietly all over the room. "I hear Storm's coming here for his men now."

An animal snarl from the crowd answered this last remark.

"Nobody gets away from the Company," somebody near Rick said. "How come yuh managed it?"

Rick held out his wrists. "See those marks? You think I was wearing shackles for the fun of it?" He spoke to the crowd. "Yeah, I was lucky. I got away down an abandoned drift. But the others didn't. You know what they used on us? A Banning, full power. I've seen what happens to the guys the Company takes! I've lived in the barracks and sweated in the mines and had the living blazes kicked out of me, right along with them. I was lucky. Now I'm telling you. Unless we do something about Jaffa Storm and that gang of his, we'll all die in the pits before we're through!"

"Sure," said Texas, after the noise had died down. "But Storm holds all the aces, Rick. I'd shore like to tromp his head in, but can anyone get inside to do it?"

"I can," Rick said.

He watched the men lean forward hungrily. "Listen, you guys! Maybe you know there was some trouble in the Old Town a few nights ago. Well, I was there. I saw Storm march his men in and blast down their king and a bunch of Marshie leaders. The Marshies are going to hit the Company tonight, with everything they've got. Are you going to let them have all the fun?"

He waited until he could make himself heard again.

"And I'm telling you this, too! Unless we fight along with the Marshies, we're done. And why shouldn't we? Gosh, they're human too, and we've both taken it from the Company long enough! We're going to have to fight the Company sooner or later. How long do you think the little guys like us can last on Mars, fighting Storm and the Marshies both?"

He let them think about that, for a moment.

"I've got it fixed to get inside the compound tonight," he said quietly. "I owe Jaffa Storm a big debt, and I aim to pay it off. How many of you guys want to be there when we open the gates?"

The air was full of waving fists and a great harsh roar.

"You take 'em, Tex," Rick said. "Get 'em there fast, and quiet. Keep separate from the Marshies until the fighting begins, but work with them. I got that end all fixed. Get volunteers to take up what 'copters and atmoplanes there are in this dump and clean out the Bannings by the gates. Take every weapon you can scrape up, if I don't manage to do what I'm planning to do, you and the Marshies can kick the gates down, anyway, together!"

At the same moment Kyra had been trying to win cooperation from the Martians with but meager results. The thief in the golden rags was scowling sullenly. He was proving stubbornly antagonistic.

"Earthmen!" sneered the thief. "When men spill blood together in the same cause, it makes them brothers. Should we become brothers to them?"

The men around the table let out a yell.

"No!" they shrieked. There were five of them, representing every Quarter and class in Ruh.

Kyra beat the air impatiently with her wings.

"These Earthmen have done you no harm," she said. "They mean you no harm. They've suffered from the Company as much as you have, and they have a blood debt. By our own laws, can we deny them the right to pay it?"

The men thought about that. The thief started to say something. Kyra spoke first.

"Together, Martians and Earthmen both, we can destroy the Company. We'll have weapons, and strength. Alone either one of us would fail. This, even if—if Rick should be killed, we can go ahead and win." She waited a moment, and then cried out, "The Earthmen will go, whether we do or not! Will you let them have all the glory?"

The men around the table rose and howled that they would not.

"We'll fight!" they bellowed. "Down with the Company!"

CHAPTER IX

AFTER a search Rick found St. John and Eran Mak on the 'copter field just beyond the shacks of the town.

"You fix it with Storm all right?" Rick asked.

"Yes," answered St. John. "Told him I had news from the Polar Cities—something so important to him and Fallon that I was scared stiff. Don't know whether he believed me or not."

"Doesn't matter, as long as we get there."

More time passed. Noise, movement, and light died in the New Town. St. John threw down the stub of his cigarette.

"Time now, Rick?"

"Yeah. Let's go."

They climbed into the neat little flier. Eran Mak took one last look at the sky.

"The moons are right together, Rick," he said. "Favorable omen for Mars. Chance, or did you plan it that way?"

"What do you think? Shut the door, for Pete's sake, and let's go!"

Because he was looking for them, Rick saw the crowds of men moving across the sea-bottom from Ruh. They went without lights, spread out widely, hugging the shadows. Rick hoped that owing to the rough terrain and the confusing moonlight they could get close to the Company walls without being spotted.

The Company compound was blazing with light, everything going full blast. While they watched, two ships went up from the port, trailing comet-tails of flame across the night. The little 'copter trembled in the air-wash the rocket-liners left behind them.

"Wait a minute!" Rick said suddenly. The others looked at him, startled. He was watching the rocket-flares. "How do I know?" he muttered. "Storm read our minds before. How do I know?" He burst without warning into a rowdy ballad about a spaceman's daughter and a lonesome comet, shoved St. John away from the controls, and took over himself. His eyes blazed with excitement.

"Have you gone crazy?" St. John snapped.

But Eran Mak studied Rick shrewdly.

"There are more things in heaven and Mars than you Earth-born people know," he said. "Telepathy, for one." He glanced quickly at the way the 'copter was heading now. "Come on, Hugh. Let's sing!"

Using the ballad as a screen for his thoughts, Rick shot the 'copter toward the spaceport and brought it low over a dark and deserted area on its outskirts. Then he handed the controls back to St. John.

"Storm may not have been as busy as I thought," he explained. "He may have picked my mind clean, for all I know, and set a trap for us all. Anyway, I got a better idea, and a better chance of getting by with it. Get back to the men, double quick, and tell 'em to stay way back from the Company until I'm through. Then come in swinging!"

"How will we know when you're through?"

"You'll know!"

St. John frowned, looking quickly at the spaceport. Rick's jaw hardened.

"He isn't running out, Hugh," Eran Mak said quietly. "Let's go."

"Sorry," St. John said curtly.

Rick grunted and dropped out the door, ten feet or so to the ground. The 'copter speed away. Rick stood still, looking around him, and then headed for the loom of a row of launching racks about a half mile away. Apparently no one had noticed the furtive landing. There was no reason why anyone should have, at that distance from the field.

From the small size of the racks he judged the ships cradled there were private jobs belonging to officials of the Company. That was exactly what Rick wanted. Everything was dark around them, too, which meant that nobody was going anywhere just now.

Rick crawled face downward for the last few hundred yards. That was fortunate, because he avoided the electric-eye warning beams, which were set to catch a man knee-height from the ground. Presently he was in the shadow of one of the huge tilted tubes. The racket of the port itself, where men slaved to load Fallonite and unload supplies, was close to him.

The rack was not locked. There was no reason to keep it locked. Rick slid inside, through the double-lock into the cradled ship. A nice, opulent, easy-to-handle baby, convertible for atmosphere travel. Sweating with the need for haste, Rick found a bulger in the locker and put it on. Then he strapped himself into the pilot's seat and got busy.

The thunder of the warming motors must have brought people running, but Rick didn't wait to see.

He took off long before the tubes were safely heated, and once a spaceship has begun thundering there isn't much anyone can do about it.

He made a long screaming arc upward clear of the thin air-blanket. Then he flipped over, got the rotos going, and swooped back toward the Company compound. On the way he dumped fuel, watching the gauge carefully. Mayo's bungalow prison was way off from the Administration pylon, but he was taking no chances.

He came in high and pushed the ship's nose downward, aiming it like a bomb over the pylon and the north wall. Then he locked the controls, pushed the ignition wide open, and bailed out, blasting blue blazes out of the bulger-rocket to get away from there.

The force of the explosion threw him around, even so. It was beautiful. The pylon crumpled down like a dropped wedding cake, and the walls flattened outward. After that everything was hidden by smoke and flying debris.

Rick smiled, his teeth glinting wolf-like in the moonlight. Then he changed his course, shooting away toward the far side of the compound where Mayo was.

On the way he saw men pouring up out of the folds and creases of the sea-bottom, flowing toward the breached walls. Earthmen and Martians, running together over the gray moss, blasters and slice-bars swinging beside sword-blades and the spiked knuckle-dusters of the Low-Canals. Just men, now, carrying the same hate in their hearts, charging the same barricade.

Rick nodded. "Make 'em bleed together," he thought, "and you've made brothers. For a while, at least. And a while is all I need."

He dropped down, into the dark and quiet back lot of the compound, and found Mayo's bungalow from Kyra's verbal map. He climbed out of the heavy bulger, laughing at the weakness of his knees and the way his heart pounded. Excitement of the ship and the wrecking, sure, but there was more to it than that.

The bungalow was unlocked. He knew the minute he opened the door that it was empty. He went through the rooms, calling Mayo's name, and then he saw the blood on the carpet, a trail of it, fresh and wet. He turned cold, and very quiet.

He followed the erratic spatter of red drops across the paving outside, to a little shed that might have housed a 'copter, kept secretly for an emergency. The trail ended there.

Rick ran back. He yelled for Kyra, but there was no answer, though he had sent her to watch, to help Mayo escape if she could. There was a tremendous roar of fighting now, where Storm's Venusians were standing off the Terro-Martian rabble. Rick ran toward it, more slowly now because the wounds in his feet were making themselves felt. On the way he saw the prison-barracks of the work-gangs had been thrown open according to his instructions.

Things were a little confused for Rick after that. He was caught up in the fighting, but he only half saw the men he blasted down. He was looking for St. John and Eran Mak—not because he wanted them, but because he wanted their 'copter. He was thinking of Mayo and Jaffa Storm, and he was not quite sane.

Between the men of Ruh, New Town and Old, and the liberated slaves, the Company resistance was crushed, utterly. Rick's stunt with the crashing ship had almost done it alone, and without Storm to egg them on the Venusians were weakened. It was quiet again in a surprisingly short time. At last Rick found St. John and Eran Mak standing at the edge of the enormous crater made by Rick's ship. The ruined pylon lay like a giant scrap pile over one edge. The two men were bending over a twisted metal object.

"Heaven only knows," St. John was saying. "I never saw anything like it before. But it's probably just as well we didn't have to face it."

Eran Mak touched it, shivering slightly. "It was made for death. You can feel that." He saw Rick then, started to hail him, and changed it to a startled, "What's wrong?"

"Mayo. Storm's taken her—had a 'copter hidden out. Where's yours?"

"Won't fly," said St. John briefly. "Debris hit the prop." His face was white and strained, suddenly. "We'll find a telescreen and get the MPG busy right away. Also the Interplanetary authorities. He may get away from Mars, but he'll be caught when he lands." He caught Rick's look of leashed fury and flinched. "It's all we can do right now! Come on."

They found a screen in the laboratory, which was untouched by the blast. While St. John made his reports, Rick paced restlessly, limping with pain but unable to sit down. They were alone in the office, the three of them. Eran Mak leaned against the door, smoking, watching Rick with hard, speculative eyes.

St. John switched off the screen. "Now. Let's talk business," he said.

"The blazes with business," snarled Rick. "I'm interested in Mayo."

Rick's mouth twitched in a half smile. "They're my men. I brought 'em together, and I control them."

He hit the collar of Ruh with his knuckle. "There's no law on Mars but strength. Storm knew that, too. Now I've got the strength. I'm willing to play along with you, unless you get under my feet too much, and I'm not going to run things the way Storm did."

"Until you have to," St. John said, "or until you feel like it. Mars is your plaything now, is that it?"

Rick's face hardened, his cold cat-gaze turned inward.

"I told Mayo I'd give her Mars to wear on a chain around her neck," he said. "I don't know what I'm going to do with it, yet, aside from that. Whatever looks the best to me. But the devil with Mars, and you, too!" He limped over to the screen, reaching for the switch. "Maybe I can get a 'copter from the field."

He heard Eran Mak's bells chiming faintly, and then in a sudden jangle of music. He turned around. The wounds in his hands and feet made him clumsy, but even so his blaster was almost drawn when Eran Mak took him across the temple with the heavy barrel of his own weapon. Rick sagged to the floor and lay still.

St. John licked his lips. "You shouldn't have done that, Mak," he said hoarsely.

"Why not?" The Martian was perfectly composed, tying Rick with brisk efficiency. "The big boy is as irresponsible as a child and just about as safe to play with as a tiger. Think for yourself what Mars will be like in five years, under his rule."

St. John nodded slowly. "A barbarian emperor has never brought anything except war and cruelty. But without Rick we'd never have won."

"No. But he did that for himself. Not for you, nor me, nor Mars." Mak rose and stood scowling at Rick, swinging the bells back and forth with his fingertip.

"What to do with him is the sticker. I don't want to kill him and there is his personal following to think about. That cursed Collar!" Mak snapped his fingers suddenly. "Get me some acid out of the lab. I can get the lock open with that. Without the Collar Rick is nothing to the Martians, and if we tell the Earthmen that Rick ran out on them with several million credits of the Company funds, it'll finish him for good."

"That's dirty, Mak!" St. John protested.

"Sometimes," said the Martian patiently, "a dirty blow wins a clean fight. Think of Mars, not Richard Gunn Urquhart. Go on, Hugh! Move!"

Hugh St. John moved.

CHAPTER X

IT TOOK Richard Gunn Urquhart a long time to collect himself. He came to slowly, in a series of mental jerks. From that, and the pendulum sensation in his head and the dead-frog taste in his mouth, he knew he'd been drugged with tsamo, a Martian narcotic.

The roof over him, when he could see it, turned out to be the ceiling of a spaceship's cabin. Through long training, Rick's subconscious did a quick weighing and sorting of the sounds filtering in from outside. The ship was in port, lading, and not yet cradled.

He felt shaky. He was in no rush to wake up—until he discovered that his right wrist was manacled to the bunk stanchion. After that, things began to come back to him. The tsamo made him stupid. Connected thinking brought the sweat of physical effort to his skin, but finally he had the pieces put together, well enough. He sat up, yelling, shaken and blazing-eyed with fury—and desperation.

No one answered. The cabin door was closed, and he was alone. He fought the cuff-chain for a while, gave it up, and subsided into a quietness that had nothing of peace in it.

He saw the letter, propped on the table beside the head of his bunk.

It was addressed to him. He tore it open.

Rick:
This is admittedly a dirty trick, but you left us no choice. The future of a world was more important than you, or us; so—

Fifty thousand credits have been placed to your account in the New York Main Office of the First Interplanetary Bank of Earth. Perhaps that will help to poultice the bump on your head. Don't try to come back to Mars. Both Martians and Terrans have been given a slanderous but logical account of your actions and will probably shoot you on sight. Moreover, as you said, there is no law on Mars but strength—and now we have the strength. Be sensible, and keep your head where it will be of use to you. Good luck.

Eran Mak.

There was also a postscript.

Don't worry about Mayo. We're moving heaven and Mars to help her.

Rick's lips pulled back from his teeth in a snarl. He crumpled the letter and threw it away. Quite suddenly he was violently sick. He lay quiet for a while, cold yet dripping sweat. The dulled racket of lading flowed past his ears, engines, winches, men yelling, the thump and crash of heavy loads.

He pulled himself up and began bellowing again.

Presently a boy came in, carrying a tray. He was like a million ship's boys on the Triangle. His ragged slops flagged loosely on his ankles and his face had a look of habitual wariness, like that of a hunted but vicious animal. He set the tray down, keeping out of Rick's reach.

"Where am I?" Rick asked.

"Jekkara Port." The kid studied him, obviously impressed by Rick's size and mature toughness.

"What ship?"

"The *Mary Ellen Dow,* outbound for Earth. We take off in three-four hours."

Despite the handcuff Rick stood up. "That means they start cradling in just a few minutes, and after that I'm stuck! Get me the skipper."

"Not a chance. No one ain't comin' in her but me, till after take-off. That's orders. 'Sides, they're busy." The boy turned toward the door again, but his attention lingered on Rick's bandaged, big brown hand.

Rick relaxed. He pointed to a purple bruise under the kid's eye and grinned. "I see you got some battle scars, too. Over a dame, I'll bet."

It was no dame. The cook had a hangover. But the kid expanded with pride.

"Yeah," he said. "Some dish, too. Happened at Madame Kan's. Ever been there?"

"You bet. Best place on Mars."

"It's okay," said the kid condescendingly. "But I don't like these Martian babes much. Too skinny."

96

"That's right. Bad tempered, too." Rick winced. "Golly, what a head I got! Who doped me?"

"I dunno. You was out cold when they carried you in. That was three days ago. You musta taken a deep breath, all right!"

"I guess so." That wasn't hard to figure. Eran Mak had knocked him out and then kept him that way with drugs. It must have been Eran Mak, then, who had taken the Collar of Ruh. Rick gave the boy a sudden look of intimate intentness. "Kick that door shut and come over here. I want to talk to you."

"I ain't got the key to that cuff on me."

"I know that. Listen, pick up that letter and read it."

The boy obeyed, warily. His eyes began to bulge. "Fifty thousand credits!" he said hoarsely. "My stars!"

"You could buy Madame Kan's, with that."

"No," said the kid softly. He was looking way off somewhere, and his face changed. "No. I'd get my master's ticket and then I'd buy my own ship—or part of it. A ship that would maybe go out—clear out to The Belt and even Jupiter."

"You can have it, kid."

The boy turned around and looked at him. His mouth twisted sullenly. He started to go out.

"I mean it," Rick said. "Listen, you fuzz-tailed sap! I'm playing for something bigger than fifty thousand measly credits. If I don't get off this ship before she starts cradling, I'll lose something plenty important. I'm offering to buy the key to this handcuff for fifty thousand credits."

The kid stared at him. He tried three times before he could get the words out. "Ain't got the key."

"I've been a ship's boy myself. You can get it."

The kid ran his hands through his hair and across his face. He seemed to be having trouble breathing. "I ain't fallin' for no bunk like that!" he cried out suddenly. "I'll get eight bells beat out of me for lettin' you go, and that's all I'll get."

"Gimme that letter." Rick went through his pockets and found a stub of pencil. The boy tossed the wadded paper on the bunk, still not coming close. "What's your name?"

"Yancey, William Lee Yancey."

Rick smoothed out the letter and wrote carefully on the back of it. Then he tossed it back. The kid read haltingly:

To whom it may concern. William Lee Yancey has done a job for me worth fifty thousand credits. My account in the First Interplanetary Bank of Earth, New York Main Office (see other side), is to go to William Yancey.

Richard Gunn Urquhart.

A slow, hot glow came into the boy's eyes. He rolled the paper tight and hid it on him.

"Wait," he said, and went out.

Rick waited. He waited a thousand years, and his heart wore a hole through his ribs. He stared at the cabin wall, but all he could see was Mayo's face the last time he remembered it, with the sweat and blood of his impalement glistening, jewel-like, on the white skin and the dark eyes full of sorrow and terror and love.

The kid came back, and he had the key.

"Swiped it out of the Skipper's extra pants," he grinned. "They're hookin' the tugs on. We got to hurry."

Rick could hear the powerful electro-magnets of the roaring tugs clamping onto the ship's skin, ready to wrestle her into her launching cradle. The job would take several hours, but after it was started there was no way on or off.

The lock clicked. Rick flung the cuff off and they went to the door. There was no one in the corridor. Officers were on the bridge, crew strapped into their launching hammocks. Sometimes the cradling was tougher on the crew than the take-off.

The warning bell rang through the ship. Air locks were already shut. The boy pulled Rick's sleeve. "Waste chute," he said. "This way." They ran. Rick's feet were still stiff and sore, but he could use them all right.

They found the chute, slid in, and let the compressed air blow them gently out. The tugs made a deafening clamor, heaving and straining to shift the huge bulk. Nobody noticed the two men running from the shadows under the hull of the Mary Ellen Dow. It was not quite dawn, with Diemos dying in the western sky and the sun not born yet in the east.

Rick paused in the shelter of a towering empty cradle, and saw that the boy had disappeared. Rick smiled crookedly.

"Didn't trust me not to clip him and take my letter back," he thought. "Yeah. Well, he's smart, at that."

He promptly forgot the kid and the fifty thousand credits in deciding what was the safest and quickest way to steal a 'copter. In his spaceman's dress he could get by all right unless Eran Mak and St. John had plastered his description around too much on the telescreen. Finally he shrugged. That was a chance he'd have to take.

He walked on, erect and not too fast, acting as

though he belonged there. He only stopped once, to pick up a piece of heavy scrap that fitted nicely into his curled-up fingers. There was about him a cold, withdrawn look—of ruthless concentration.

The 'copter field was a good mile and a half from the rocket field. Jeeps sped back and forth between them and the huge warehouses, sheds, and repair shops. Even at this early hour Jekkara Port was awake and hustling. Before long, one of the jeeps slowed down and the driver offered Rick a lift.

Refusal would have been more dangerous than acceptance—spacemen never walk if they can help it. Rick climbed aboard.

The driver, an indistinct dark shape in the gloom, talked as he sent the little car bucketing across toward the 'copter field.

"You just in, pal?"

"Yeah."

"Then you ain't heard the news, I guess."

"No."

"Well, the Terran Exploitations Company has had the blinking stuffings knocked out of it. Some of our guys finally got smart and took the law in their own hands. Looked like for a while the Company was gonna own the whole cussed planet, but now us little guys are gonna have a look-in. Swell deal, all around. This new gover'ment they're putting together is all right."

He burst into sudden laughter. "Only thing is, we got to get in harness with the Marshies. Well, it's their world—and if they let me pick my own, I won't mind!"

"Yeah," said Rick. "That's fine."

"Suits me." The light was getting stronger now, with the suddenness of Martian dawns. "Funny thing about that Urquhart bird, though. Rick, they call him. Fed everybody a lot of pious bunk about the future of Mars. Got the fight going, and then ran out on his pals with about everything in the Company's safe. Took a collar with him, too—some gimmick that's sacred to the Marshies, or something. He better never come back to Mars if he wants to stay healthy."

Rick said nothing. The 'copter field was still too far away.

The driver rattled on. "Lots of guys is going to buy land here. Build cities, make the earth good again. Yeah, there's a great future from Terra. There'll be a lot of work to do, and it'll mean something when we get through. Why, my boy might be President of the MPG some day!" He turned to Rick. "Why don't you grab yourself a piece of this? Ain't no future in space except old age and the grav-bends . . ."

"His voice trailed off. His eyes got wide. "Hey," he said. "Hey, you're—you're—Rick!"

Rick hit him with his loaded fist. But the driver was tough, too, and quick. He was half stunned in spite of his rapid twist, but he fell across the horn and made it bleat like a scared goat—a goat enlarged to the size of a small spaceship. Drivers in other jeeps began to slow down and look around.

Rick kicked the guy clear out onto the ground and grabbed the wheel himself. Somebody yelled. More horns began to blare. Jeeps circled around, whipping red veils of dust behind them. Rick jammed his foot down on the throttle.

The dregs of the tsamo in his system wiped out all the emotions in him other than his main determination to get where he was gong. Only a complete lunatic could have got away with it. He did. He

101

shot full speed toward the 'copter field, horn and throttle pressed wide open, and left it to the other men to get out of his way.

They did. Some of them so narrowly that a sheet of tissue paper would have been torn between the passing wheels, but they did. They weren't quite crazy enough to stand against the driver who didn't care whether they stood or not.

Rick crashed through onto the edge of the 'copter field. By this time there were alarms ringing and men running around, but nobody was quite sure yet what the trouble was. There was a sleek, fast little ship warming up out on the tarmac. Rick went for it. Three startled mechanics scattered away from his jeep. Rick jumped out and let it tear on by itself.

The owner of the 'copter came from the other side of the ship. The mechanics closed in. There was a lot of noise. Rick hunched his shoulders, still cuddling the hunk of scrap in his fist. He knocked two of the mechanics cold. The third was too dizzy to get up, and the owner took one look at Rick and ran away.

Rick was clear of the ground before anyone else could get close enough to do anything.

He pushed the motor wide open, heading for a low range of hills in the distance. Other 'copters, six or seven of them, were shooting up from the field behind him in furious pursuit. Rick spared one hand for the telescreen. He listened briefly and then smiled, not because anything was funny.

His escape from the *Mary Ellen Dow* had been discovered, and the skipper was screaming to high heaven about it. The driver of the jeep had been revived sufficiently to tell who slugged him, and the field dispatcher was sending out a general alarm over the theft of the 'copter.

Such calls were addressed variously to the Martian Planetary Patrol and to Hugh St. John. Rick had never known anything on Mars to move that fast. The driver had been right—there was considerable feeling about that Urquhart guy, and none of it was friendly.

Rick left his screen on as an aid to keeping track of what Mars was doing about him. Angry, red-faced men tried repeatedly to make him answer direct calls. He left his transmitter off and didn't even bother to curse them privately.

The pursuing ships hung right on his tail, but he had played in luck. There wasn't anything there good enough to overhaul him. The hill swept up under him, worn and red and barren, scarred with hollow canyons like cavities in an old man's teeth. Rick's tawny brows got a deep cleft between them.

His pursuers couldn't catch him, but he couldn't get away. His position had been radioed all over Mars, and pretty soon there would be MPP ships circling in, and probably a few of St. John's. All landing fields where he might go for fuel would be warned and closed against him. The 'copter didn't look like it was going to be much help to him.

He thought all that over, studying the landscape —screwed up tight inside but not panicky. Just coldly weighing his chances.

There began to be calls in quick Martian rattling through his receiver. MPP men signaling position, and getting close.

Far away down the tired line of hills Rick was a red cloud rolling in from the desert. He let his breath out in what might have been a laugh and kicked the rudder bar. The little ship made a tight arc across the sky, fled screaming, and plunged a few moments later into the heart of a sandstorm.

CHAPTER XI

DEEP into the sandstorm plunged Rick's 'copter! It was one of those howling, angry khamsins that burst up from nowhere when the lonesome winds meet each other and start quarreling. They had swept up over the hills now, swirling their dusty cloaks in each other's faces. Anything less scientifically stabilized than the 'copter would have been smashed into the ground within ten minutes. But the little craft took the punishment bravely, bounding wildly in the twisting currents, going where they pushed her, but riding them, her automatic stabilizers keeping her level. Rick set the controls and locked them. She'd fly on all right, all by herself.

There was a standard emergency escape kit in the rack. He strapped the harnass around him, tied a thick cloth tightly over his face, and dropped through the hatch.

He fell into stifling sheets of sand. They wrapped themselves around him, crushed and beat and tore him, worked into his clothes and into his eyes and mouth and nose. He pressed the plunger on the escape rig. He was dropping fast, too fast. In the roar of the storm he couldn't hear whether or not the lighter-than-hydrogen synthetic gas was going into the balloon or not. Seeing anything much was out of the question.

After a while his rate of descent slackened and he was conscious of pressure by the harness. Relief brought a quick cold sweat on him. He thought about back in the old days when a guy had to depend on a chute for a low altitude jump, and thanked Providence whoever it was that thought up the synthesilk balloon which could be inflated in three seconds from a pressure tank and a man could live through almost anything there was in the sky.

The 'copter would head empty out of the storm and with any luck the hounds would waste a lot of time chasing her. By that time Rick could have lost himself in the hills—providing the wind didn't slam him flat against a cliff he couldn't see.

It didn't, quite. The balloon bobbed out suddenly toward the edge of the storm. Noting the difference in the light, Rick uncovered his eyes, shielding them with his hands and peering through the merest slits. Dimly, very dimly like the shadow of a submerged rock under his feet, he saw a ragged pinnacle, and then ahead of him a vast looming shape that looked solid.

He doubled his knees into his chest and took the impact as he would have taken a fall, on his flexed legs. It jarred him badly, but no more. He pulled on the cord that let gas out of the bag, clinging desperately to the eroded rock. The wind dragged at the balloon, and the balloon dragged at his harness, and pretty soon his fingers were bleeding with hanging on, but he hung. In a minute or two the deflated bag flapped down around him.

It didn't weigh much, only a couple of pounds.

Rick eased with infinite care out of the harness and let it drop. Then he just hugged the rock and waited.

The storm went away as suddenly as it had come, leaving drifts of red dust in the sheltered places—partly from the desert, partly dropped in the wind's fresh gnawing of the eroded cliffs. The sky was empty of ships. Down below him there was a ravine, with little tangled canyons leading out of it—leading to anywhere you wanted to go, to nowhere, to death.

Rick judged the position of the sun with great care, and began to climb down.

He reached the floor of the ravine without trouble, chose a canyon that extended in the direction he desired to go, and started to walk. He walked as silently as possible, stopping frequently to listen. In his former visits and his association with Martian space-rats, he had picked up a working knowledge of who —or what—lived where on the planet.

This was Shunni country, and had been vaguely something else before. "Before," on Mars, means a long, long time. Somewhere ahead, beyond the foothills, was the Low-Canal town of Valkis, and the whole area had been intensely Pan-Martian. Rick didn't know how they'd feel about the Collar of Ruh, here on the other side of the planet. He could guess their sentiments about an Earthman, however. Any Earthman, but especially one named Richard Gunn Urquhart.

The canyon twisted aimlessly. It was hot. It was dry. Rick's tongue began to swell, with a taste like mouldy feathers. There had been no water on the 'copter—evidently the mechanics had not finished servicing her. His feet began to throb. It was quiet.

Under the high walls of the canyon, with a narrow strip of sky overhead, it was like being dead and in the grave, but not yet buried. As time wore on, Rick began to expect a shovelful of dirt in his face any minute. The dregs of the tsamo in him did queer things to his mind.

He came finally to a sharp elbow bend. There was a cleft in the left-hand wall, like a window, and he looked out across foothill slopes at a town huddled, like an old, old woman in ochre rags, beside a sluggish, dull canal.

That was Valkis. Valkis was a bad town. It was the thieves' market, a hideout for wanted men, a sinkhole of vice, a place where a lot of women and quite a few men went and were never heard of again. But it had something, or was supposed to have something. A landing field and a couple of camouflaged hangars that concealed ships such as no honest men ever possessed. Sleek things with souped-up motors that even the MPP ships couldn't touch.

Rick studied it with hard cat-eyes. He could afford to rest a while, now. Go down the slopes with the night and the shadows, later on, and hunt. And after that—well, there'd be time to plan.

He turned around, thinking about a safe place to hide and sleep, and discovered men had silently surrounded him. He hadn't heard so much as a breath or the whisper of a sandal on rock, or the rubbing of leather harness. But they were there.

They were on both sides of him. Tall, hard-faced solemn men with blank, hard, solemn eyes, with barbed spears in their hands and knives in their belts and the animal sheen of strength in their olive skins and olive-purple har. Shunni barbarians.

Rick and the Shunni studied each other without speaking for some time. Finally one huge man pointed his chin at Valkis beyond the rock-window.

"You want to go to Valkis, Earthman-called-Rick?"

"You know me?"

"Every man on Mars knows you. The seers have sent into every village the picture of the man who united Earth and Mars."

Rick nodded. "I want to go to Valkis."

"We are like brothers to the men of Valkis," he said. "You will go there."

Rick's eyes flickered. The men began to close in, still quiet, still solemn. Rick raised his hands slowly and leaned back against the canyon wall.

"Look," he said. "I'm tired. I'm unarmed. I've had all the roughing up I want for a while. Just take it easy, and I'll be good."

They took it easy. Very easy, for barbarians with a deep and ancient hate in their souls. Too easy.

And they were as brothers to the men of Valkis.

After a while, as they wound their way down the barren foothill gorges, Rick got the idea that there was some deep emotion behind the blank solemnity of their eyes. He got the idea that they were very happy men.

They came to Valkis in the quick thin dusk. Because of the condition of Rick's feet, the Shunni had carried him most of the way, on a rude litter of spears and skin robes. It was as though they wanted him to rest and regain strength. They kept him bound.

Rick guessed that some telepathic message had preceded them. The narrow streets, the roofs of the flat stone houses and the mouths of the dark alleys between them were crowded with people. Lithe rat-faced little men dressed in gaudy rags, and their lithe little women with bells in their black braids and their ears and around their ankles, making a wicked, whispering music up and down the shadowy streets.

There was no talk, no jeering nor cursing. Rick walked erect between his Shunni guards, and the Martians watched him with their eyes of emerald and topaz—slanted eyes that showed no white around the iris—and nobody made a sound. The last of the light ran westward out of the sky, and then, in the darkness, a drum began to beat.

It came from somewhere ahead, in the center of the town. It boomed out six times with crisp authority, and was silent. As though it were a signal, the crowd began to flow into the street behind the Shunni, following, without speaking. The tinkling of the bells ran like canorous laughter in the stillness.

The drum sounded again, six more single blows. Then, abruptly, harps came thrumming in, the queer little double-banked things they play along the Low-Canals, that have such an unhealthy sympathy with human nerves that they act more like drugs than music. The drum began an intricate throbbing to an off-beat rhythm. As one man, Valkis sucked its breath in, and let it out in a long sigh.

Richard Gunn Urquhart walked steadily, his face blank, his eyes hooded. His hands, tied behind his back were cold. Sweat trickled over his skin and presently, along the right side of his face, the muscles began to twitch.

As they entered the town, he had seen the landing field, to the north along the canal.

They came to the water suddenly, running black and sluggishly between banks of sunken stone. They turned north, and up ahead there were torches flaring orange against the night. The houses faced upon a square, the pavements of which had been worn hollow by countless generations of sandaled feet.

The drummer and the harpers were there. They were old women, wearing only a semblance of clothing, all of their bodies that were uncovered, without paint or ornamentation, even their heads shaved clean. They were lost in a ritual dance, their eyes glazed, their leathery shoulders twitching sharply as they breathed.

They crouched in a semi-circle around a gigantic slab of stone, raised no more than twelve inches above the ground level and polished black as though many hands had stroked it. Stone steps led down, under it.

Rick's gaze stabbed briefly around, looking for a way out and not finding it. Too many people, too much strength. He would have to wait until they untied his hands and removed the long hobble that let him walk, but not run. The Shunni had not, for one second, given him the slightest chance to escape.

They took him down the steps.

He began to remember things he had heard about the gods of Valkis. Just talk, the idle scuttlebutt of the space ways. Valkis kept its secrets well. But people talked, anyway, and what they said wasn't pretty.

They went down a long way in the dark and came out in a long square-roofed place that looked like a temple. The roof was supported with squat stone pillars. The first thing Rick noticed was the heat. Mars is a cold world, and down here it was as hot as Venus. Fires burned on round brick platters between the lines of pillars, tended by more of the shaven hags.

There was something more than fire. There was steam. He could hear the hiss of water over hot rock somewhere, from a hidden inlet from the canal.

Stifling clouds of it drifted around, making the stones and the people glisten with sweat. The music was faint now, hardly more than an echo.

The mob flowed on around a huge pit sunk in the floor of the temple. It was about twelve feet deep. It was empty. It was clean. There were four doors in the walls, closed with curtains of crimson silk.

The Shunni halted Rick at the edge of the pit, and then for the first time somebody spoke.

A man, who might have been the mayor of Valkis, or the high priest, or both, came and stood in front of Rick. He looked the Earthman up and down, and the sheer distilled hate was almost like a visible aura.

"Look at him," the man whispered, staring at Rick. "Look at him!"

The stone walls took the whisper and played with it, so that every person in there could hear. They all looked.

"The Shadow over Mars! The shadow of outland rule, the shadow of death for our world and our people. Look at him! A thief and a liar—the man who put the yoke on our necks and nailed it there! But for him, there would have been no union."

A sound ran through the place like a wolf licking its teeth.

Rick smiled, not because he felt like smiling.

"It's too bad for you, isn't it?" he said. "As soon as the new government is set, they'll clean you out of here like a nest of roaches. I don't wonder you're sore. The old way of no law at all was so much nicer."

The little man stepped back and kicked Rick with a diabolical accuracy below the belt.

"Untie the Earthman," he said. "Drop him into the pit. Drop him gently."

Once more, the Shunni were very, very kind. . . .

111

CHAPTER XII

GIDDY and winded, Rick crouched on the stones, getting his wind back. Faces peered down at him, wreathed in the coiling steam. Once again there was silence. This time it was a hungry thing, crouched and waiting.

It was hot, with the heavy oppressive heat of a low jungle. The air was dead, unstirring, acrid with sweat. Now there began to be another odor under that. A rich dark smell of rotten earth—earth fattened with other things than dirt. A smell utterly alien to the dry thin air of Mars, where cactus and brittle scrub is all that grows.

Then he discovered the perfume.

It stole through and over the coarser smells clear and poignant as the single note of a violin above the basses. It was faint, as though with distance, and yet it set all Rick's nerves to quivering.

It was like the perfume the girls wear on the Street of Nine Thousand Joys, if you could take it off the body and put it on the soul. It promised all the sensual pleasures he knew, and a few he didn't know, and still there was nothing crude about it. It was the kind of perfume angels would wear while they were making love, spreading sweetness from the shaken silver feathers of their wings.

He was still all alone in the pit, and there was still no sound. The crimson curtains hung motionless.

Rick's mouth tightened angrily. He glanced, without letting them see that he did, at the faces rimming

the pit. They were expectant, waiting, the eyes unwinking, the mouths sucking shallow breaths over
teeth bared and glistening to the firelight. They'd
been here before, and they knew what was coming.

It was the waiting that got you. The silence, and
the wondering. The muscles began to jerk again along
his right cheek. He stood erect, and walked delib-
erately to the center of the pit. Then slowly so that
they could see that his hands were steady, he put a
cigarette in his mouth, lighted it, and drowned the
match-flame in a long, easy plume of smoke.

That impressed them, a lot more than he'd
dreamed. There was no tobacco on Mars, no climate
nor soil to grow it. Smoking was still a new and
startling thing.

A few of the Martians began to cough. The fumes
were clinging heavily to the misty air, and their
throats weren't used to it. Rick grinned and blew
some more their way.

A sharp sigh sped around the pit suddenly, and
the faces swayed inward. It had nothing to do with
the cigarette. They were looking at something behind
Rick.

He whirled and saw Mayo McCall standing there
across from him, as though she had just stepped
through the silken curtains.

She wore the torn, green coverall that bared her
throat and shoulder, the dregs of the firelight poured
red glints into her hair. There was sweat on her face,
and drops of blood. She looked at him, and all her
heart was in her eyes.

Rick's lips parted, but no sound came. He stood
staring for a moment, and then he moved toward her
—slowly at first, then more rapidly, until he was al-

113

most running. His bandaged hands reached out, and all at once there were tears on his cheeks.

"I love you, Rick," Mayo whispered, and stepped back through the curtains, and was gone.

Rick cried her name and ripped the crimson silk away. There was a shallow niche beyond it. It was empty, and the solid stones mocked him with the sound of his own voice. He beat on them.

"Mayo!" he screamed, and the Martians let go a feral howl of laughter.

Rick turned around, half crouched and snarling. His eyes blazed crazily. That was what they'd been waiting for. That was part of the game.

"Mayo, Mayo!" his soul seemed to cry. "Where did you go, how did you get here, why did you run away?"

The sides of the pit were swimming before his eyes, as though he were drunk. The heat, cursed heat! The perfume!

"Steady down, Richard Gunn Urquhart!" he heard himself say. "Steady—or you'll make a fool of yourself!"

He was swaying on his feet, but he didn't know it. He discovered he was still holding the cigarette. The bandages held his fingers close together so it hadn't dropped out. He took another drag on it. The smoke did something—he didn't know whether it was better or worse. Anyway, it killed the lovely effluvium of that wretched perfume.

He saw movement out of the corner of his eye and turned to find Kyra standing in the second doorway.

She stood on tiptoe, her wings outspread. They, and her huge dark eyes, held deep opaline lights. She was smiling, and in her hands was the Collar of Ruh.

A thin animal wail went up from the watching Martians—sheer hate made vocal. It touched an answering chord in Rick. The Collar grew large before his eyes, dwarfing Kyra, dwarfing the pit. It became as large as Mars. It was Mars.

"I know the prophecy—your shadow over Mars," Kyra said. "Life to Mars, instead of death. Your life —you live so strongly."

Rick hardly heard her. His blood beat thunderously inside his skull. Kyra, Mayo, everything was drowned in a hot flood of desire. Mars, Power, wealth, Richard Gunn Urquhart the space-rat made into the guy at the top of the heap.

He laughed up at the Martians, savage laughter, and taunted them with the filth of three worlds and a dozen dialects. The dull iron bosses of the Collar blinked redly, like somnolent eyes. Dying Mars, awaiting the conqueror.

He reached out to take the Collar.

It slipped through his fingers. Kyra smiled and vanished through the curtains.

Again Rick cried out and wrenched the hangings down. Again there was nothing but a shallow niche and emptiness, and hard stone under his hands.

And once again the Martians laughed.

Rick taggered back to the center of the pit. He did not cry out now, nor curse. He looked with narrow, empty eyes at the faces peering down, the dark fresco of them above him in the steam, studded with hot jewels and the white glitter of teeth. He was afraid.

The perfume stroked his olfactory nerves with fingers of soft flame. It was pleasant. It sent ripples of sensuous delight through him. Yet because it was a part of what was being done to him he feared it, and especially so because it was pleasant. The animal was close to the surface in Rick, and it spoke.

"Bait for the trap," it said.

He raised the hand that held the cigarette, and it was not until then that he realized he was on all fours. That frightened him most of all. He dragged hungrily on the butt, burning slowly in the wet air. It made him dizzy and sick, but he could stand up again.

He did, and there was a naked girl poised in front of the third door—a green-eyed wanton with coppery hair curling on her white shoulders and her red lips brimming with secret laughter. She twitched the cutains aside and beyond them Rick saw the Street of Nine Thousand Joys, bright with lanterns and the warm light spilling out of familiar doorways, human and safe with voices, quarrels, music, the smell of wine.

The Street of Nine Thousand Joys, where Richard Gunn Urquhart was just Rick the space-rat, without a prophecy, with no enemies and no destiny but tomorrow's handover. Escape.

"Go back and be just Rick again," something was telling him. "Forget Mars and the Collar and the woman named Mayo. Get good and drunk and forget, and stop tearing your head out. Above all, escape!"

The girl tossed her head and moved away, watching him over her shoulder. Rick followed. He called to her to wait, lurching unsteadily, fighting down a childish urge to cry. She shook her curly head mockingly and fled before him down the dappled shadows, and Rick ran after.

He heard the wicked scream of laughter from above him just an instant before he crashed headlong into a blank wall of stone. He dropped, stunned. The girl, the street, vanished, and there was only an empty niche like the others.

Rick lay still. Presently he began to sob, his mouth relaxed and wet like a child's.

The Martians grew silent. They were waiting again.

The perfume soothed Rick. It was like a woman's fingers, comforting. His mother's fingers. Into his mind came a picture of the fourth door. Beyond that he would find rest. That was where the perfume came from. He could go beyond that curtain into the darkness, alone and in peace. He could sleep. He could forget.

Quite slowly, he got to his hands and knees and began to crawl toward the fourth door. There was no sound anywhere now. The Martians seemed to have stopped breathing.

Something kept trying to jar Rick's mind awake again. A smell, an acrid familiar reek that clashed with the perfume. He didn't want to wake. He ignored it and went on crawling.

He came to the fourth door and thrust the crimson hangings back. Before him was a dark passageway, slanting sharply down. The perfume breathed from it, and under it, suddenly strong, the rich smell of earth. A latent memory made Rick reach out and feel the emptiness, not quite knowing why he did. The passageway was really there.

He crawled into it. The last thing he heard as the crimson draperies closed behind him was the laughter of the Martians like the spring cry of wolves on a hilltop.

It was easy to crawl, half sliding, down the slope. Presently he could sleep, and forget. . . .

Pain, a savage searing stab of it between his fingers. It shook through the drugged clouds in his brain. He tried to push it away, but it slashed and stabbed and wouldn't go, and the involuntary reflexes of his body fought to do something about it. He raised his hand, and again the acrid smell assailed him. There was a little red glow in the darkness.

The cigarette stuck between his fingers had burned down and was searing the tender flesh. The bandage was smoldering.

He pushed the butt out and hugged his hand to him. The pain helped to clear his head. Memories came back to him—the cryptic torture in the pit, the Martians watching him. Rage boiled up to help the pain. He was aware suddenly that the perfume was stronger, and a clear terror of it came to him. It was a drug, and it was going to get him under again.

Slowly he was sliding down the shaft.

He pressed his boots hard against the opposite wall and peered down. Far below was a phosphorescent glimmer, a glimpse of space. And—flowers!

White flowers, pale and lovely, swaying as though a vagrant breeze blew over them. Infinitely beautiful, breathing perfume, calling to him . . .

Yes. Calling to him. In his mind.

"Come!" they whispered. "Come and sleep!"

"What are you?" he asked. "Where do you come from?"

"There were many of us when the world was young, droned the answer. "We grew in the green jungles. We ruled Mars before man could walk erect."

118

The men of Valkis had found them, then, some time in the ancient past, a handful of them clinging on beside some sheltered volcanic spring. And they built a temple, and the flowers lived on.

They were beautiful. They were friendly. They smelled nice.

Rick slipped farther toward them. His head was swimming again.

"How did I see Mayo?" he asked the flowers. "What were those things out there?"

"We take the images uppermost in a man's mind and let him see them, the things he wants most."

The thought broke off short. "Why?" Rick asked drowsily.

"Come," said the flowers. "Come and sleep."

Sleep. The smell of the fat black earth came strong under the perfume, and the animal instinct of his body told Rick what it was fattened with.

He graced his feet frantically to stop his sliding. He was afraid. He knew, now. But it was too late. The drug had him, and he couldn't fight.

He began to slip again.

His burned hand hurt him, rubbing the rock. Cigarette burn. Tobacco. Out there in the pit, it had helped, a little. Even a little— Perhaps, being a drug, it fought the other drug. It wouldn't hurt to try.

He fumbled the pack out. His hands were clumsy from the bandages, and they shook. He dropped the pack. It slid away down the shaft and dropped among the flowers.

"Come," they said. "Come and sleep."

He hunted through his pockets. Feverishly, panting. He found one crumpled cigarette, dropped out of the pack and forgotten.

He was careful not to drop it, nor the matches.

He filled himself with the smoke, over and over. It nauseated him, but it fought the perfume, a little enough so he could think. Not clearly, but enough. Enough for him to claw his way back up the shaft, inch by inch, pressing his boots against the stone and inching his back up, digging with his nails into the irregularities of the rock, climbing with his muscles the way a snake glides on his scales, because he had to or die.

The flowers were angry. They were hungry. They hurled the perfume at him in drowsy clouds, but the harsh smoke fought it back. He reached the level space behind the curtains and lay there, shaking and exhausted. The cigarette was used up. He took to slapping his own face violently, pressing the raw burn, anything to keep his mind awake.

There was no sound outside in the temple but the faint crackling of the fires. Rick peered through the curtains. The gloating faces were gone from the pit rim. They hadn't waited. There was nothing to wait for. Nobody had ever before come back up that shaft. Rick went out and studied the walls.

The old women who tended the fires would not be watching the pit, either. They would be huddled over their bony knees in the heat, dreaming of the days when they wore little bells in their hair and had chimed the hot-eyed men into dusky chambers beside the Low-Canal.

The walls were old, old beyond counting. The blocks had settled and moved a little, so that their surface was not even. The walls could be climbed. Evidently, because the Martians were not affected, atmospheric pressure kept the perfume lower than the pit edge. He'd be safe, when he got up there.

He climbed, biting his lips to keep his drowsy brain awake.

After an eternity he reached the top and lay panting on the stones, covered with cold sweat. He began to shudder, violently. Gradually his head cleared.

It was very still in the temple, full of steam, full of shadows and wickedness. The old women crouched by their fires, dreaming, the wrinkled skin twitching across their shoulders, now and then, as though a hand stroked it. Rick began to move, through the quivering darkness behind the farthest line of pillars against the wall.

He reached the stairs and crept up them. The drummer and the harpers were gone from the square. The cruel, noisy life of Valkis was going on in the surrounding streets, but apparently this place was sacred to religion. It was deserted now.

Rick slipped quietly into the black water of the canal and began to swim northward. Lights blazed across the water here and there. Men and women thronged the bank in front of the canal-side houses. But Rick was a good swimmer, and no one saw him. He hauled out on the edge of the landing field.

There was nobody around, no reason for anybody to be around. Rick found a scrap of iron and pried the lock off the nearest hangar. There was a 'copter inside, a sleek wicked little thing with an illegal motor.

There was only one place on Mars Rick wanted to go. He went there, like a comet rushing to perihelion.

He went to Caer Hebra.

CHAPTER XIII

Caer Hebra came into Rick's view, just before sundown, its marble spires almost drowned and lost in the drifting sand. He set the 'copter down on a massive terrace, stained and cracked but still retaining its perfect symmetry, and climbed out.

Before his boots touched the ground he was surrounded by the little winged men of the island kingdom. No women greeted Rick this time. The small ivory faces of the men were stern, and their small furred hands held pencil-tubes.

Rick was not conscious of fear. He was not conscious of anything but the need in him.

"Is Kyra here?"

The leader nodded slowly. No one spoke. Many wings made a sad, silken rustling in the lonely wind. Sand etched light feathery patterns on the marble beneath their feet.

"I will see her," Rick said.

The leader nodded again.

"It is her wish, and the wish of the dying must be heeded," he said. "For that reason, Earthman, you will live to go away from Caer Hebra. Come."

The word "dying" shocked Rick. It cut through the numbness of his inner mind. He started and cried out, "Kyra!" There was no answer. The little men motioned him on. He obeyed.

She lay on a heap of soft furs, high up in a tower where she could look out across the dry sea. She held out her hands to Rick and smiled.

"I knew you would come," she said.

Rick took her hands, gently, as though they were flowers and easily crushed. "What's wrong?" he asked. "Baby, what's wrong?"

"The black Earthman burned her," said the leader, behind him. "She will not live."

Kyra's fingers tightened on him. "I followed them, Rick. You sent me to watch Mayo, and I did. I couldn't stop him from taking her, but I followed their ship. It went very fast, and I lost it, but I kept flying north and after a long time I sighted it again. I went down to it, and Jaffa Storm came out from the ice dome and saw me. But I broke the controls, Rick. With a stone I broke them, so his ship couldn't fly. And it was dark, very dark for an Earthman's eyes, so I got away."

She was drawing him down to her, as though he were too far away for her to see him clearly.

"I tried to get back to Ruh, to the Company, to find you, Rick. But I couldn't fly that far. I couldn't. I knew you'd come here, only I was so afraid it might be too late."

Rick kneeled down beside her. He looked over his shoulder at the men.

"Get out," he said.

They were angry. For a while they didn't move. Rick's yellow eyes took on a peculiar, almost phosphorescent glow. Kyra had forgotten that her people existed. Presently they turned and left.

"North," said Kyra. "North, in the Polar Cities under the ice dome."

"I wouldn't have had you do it," Rick whispered.

The rosy light fell across her face from the sunset, warming the ivory pallor. Her great eyes held a soft brilliance.

"Don't be sad for me, Rick."

He said nothing.

"I'm not sad. I haven't lived many years, but there isn't anything more I could have had from life. I've loved you, Rick, and in a way we've been mated, haven't we? I helped you to create a new world, even if it was only a little bit of help. Not many women have given life to a planet, have they, Rick?"

"No."

"I'll live in that new world. We believe in rebirth. Some day my soul will have a new body, and it will remember. It will say to me, 'I did this. With Rick, I did this.' And I will be happy."

She fumbled suddenly at the zipper of his shirt, drawing it down. She thrust her hands inside, against his chest.

"So strongly—I can feel it beating. That's Mars, Rick. So much life and strength, and we were so tired."

He bent over and kissed her. Then he stretched out beside her, holding her like a child in the curve of his arm, her head against his shoulder. She went to sleep, smiling.

The sun went down in the dry waves and Phobos came up from the western horizon as though borne on the afterglow. By the time Diemos had marched from the east to his nightly mating, Rick knew that Kyra would not be disturbed if he arose and went away.

He laid her back in her nest of furs. From some forgotten corner of his childhood the sign of the cross came unbidden. He made it and went out.

Silently the little men of Caer Hebra stood in the wind and the moonshadows and watched him take off. It was not until he had flown north for some hours that he realized why his eyes and throat were dried sea-water. . . .

He had been flying for a long, long time. He was cold and cramped, and the fuel gauge needle kept fluttering over to pat the terminal E.

The terrain below was a desert forgotten of God and man. Now, in the Martian spring, the gorges ran full with the thaw-water that fed the canals. There were mosses and lichens and a few tough flowers. But the black rock was rotted and split by time, ice, wind and water, and it looked as untouched by humanity as the Moon.

Far ahead he could see the soaring edges of the ice cap—the core that remained through every summer. He checked this course against the location of the Polar Cities, which were mapped but seldom visited. When a curious visitor did drop in, he returned with a weird tale of voices that spoke in his brain and told him, gently but unmistakable firmness to go away again. Nobody, except in ancient legend, had ever found the entrance to the ice domes under which the Cities were hidden.

Since these domes were regular in shape and never melted, even slightly, in high summer, it was assumed by some that the mysterious Thinkers kept them that way artificially. The Terran invasion of Mars was too young and too much interested in money to bother with half-legendary cities that no one had ever seen. A Martian, of course, observed the tabus with strict etiquette, and most of the few Earthmen who had heard of the Polar Cities put them down as a legend growing around a natural freak.

Rick's motor began to miss. He nursed and coaxed it onward, toward the glittering rim of ice knifing the pale sky. Presently it died altogether and no amount of cursing or praying could start it again. Rick pulled the glasses from the locker beside him and scanned the ground.

He saw the domes, three of them clustered together in a circle. They were far off, glistening like drops of water on a stone.

He still had altitude. He played the light 'copter like a glider on the wind, fighting for every inch of headway. He made it, almost. Just before he was forced to make a landing he sighted Jaffa Storm's ship on the ground, a tiny speck beside one of the domes.

He landed safely on a broad strip of rock ground flattened by moving ice, well out of sight of the domes. He was not sure that that made much difference for he was by now thoroughly convinced of Jaffa Storm's telepathic powers. But instinct and training made him go cautiously, just the same.

An area of tumbled boulders offered cover. Rick slipped and stumbled between them until, after a long time, he could look out onto the level space before the domes where Storm's 'copter was.

He had no weapon except the scrap of metal, which he had dropped into his pocket. There had been no blaster in the ship, and no way to get one.

Neither could he discover any cover. Rick walked out across the open ground. The lean Martian sunlight touched the domes. They were huge and perfectly round, and the light shone through them, pellucid and pure, like light through raindrops. High above them, shearing off half the sky, was the pale ice-green blade of the polar cap.

Nothing stirred. There was no sound. The 'copter had a desolate and forgotten look until he got close enough to see that someone had been working on it, repairing the controls. He studied them. The job had been competently done. The ship would fly.

Yet the ship was still there.

Rick looked around him, standing still beside the little ship. His ears, his eyes, the nerves of his skin were tuned so acutely that they ached.

Silence. Empty earth and the enigmatic domes like huge animals asleep and not telling their dreams to anybody. Over all the crushing impersonality of the ice and above that, the cold pale sky.

Rick shivered. His cheek muscles twitched and the lids narrowed cat-like over his yellow eyes. He went toward the nearest dome.

There were footprints in the bare ground. Many lines of them, going both ways. The mark of the left boot was light. There were no signs of Mayo's prints.

Rick followed them, walking steadily but without haste. The stories of the mental compulsion to go away returned to him. He felt no compulsion whatsoever. Either the legends lied, or something had been changed inside the domes.

He followed the footprints up to the curving clear wall, and nothing happened. Nothing at all.

He found the entrance. It was a hallway half-closed with intermeshing sheets of crystal that slid back into the ice and could not be told from it. A man could be caught between those crystal panels. He could be crushed and cut apart, or trapped unhurt to die slowly in a little shining cell.

He stood for a moment or two, listening to the stillness. Then he went in.

His footsteps rang back at him like echoes in a bell. Several times, through tricks of light and perspective, he thought the doors were sliding in. But he reached the interior safely. In spite of himself he was shaking and covered with sweat.

He was looking at a city.

It was sunk below ground level, so that he was even with the spires. It was not very big, limited to about ten thousand inhabitants. But it was the most beautiful thing Rick had ever seen, and the most unpleasant.

He'd been in the Lunar cave-cities. He'd walked through the fantastic monuments of an unknown race on Phobos, and on Venus he had seen a drowned empire under the silver sea. But this beat them all. It turned his stomach over.

The buildings were all made of the same material —a colorless plastic that took the prismatic sunlight from the dome overhead and played with it, so that the walls seemed to be full of drifting jewels. That was all right. It was the shape of the things that got you.

Wherever the Thinkers came from, whatever they were, they had eight brought with them or discovered an alien geometry. The buildings swept the eye along curves and angles that verred sickeningly toward another universe. The shapes of them, the meaning of them, gave the mind a shock. It was like the dream of a crazy surrealist painter brought to life, unhealthy and fascinating.

There was a swift musical clashing behind Rick. He turned around, and found that the way had closed behind him. There were no controls of any kind, so far as Rick could see.

He went down transparent steps to the city.

It was dead. He could feel that. The silence had been there too long, and the streets had stopped waiting. The leaning walls looked at him malevolently, not liking the echoes his feet called forth. Rick's eyes began to smolder.

He stopped abruptly, filled his lungs. "Mayo!" he yelled.

The cry broke into a million fragments and tinkled back at him with a sound of subtle laughter. He went on, holding a course for the far side of the city. From up there by the entrance he had seen another flight of shining steps and a hall, leading into the adjoining dome.

He wondered if Jaffa Storm had let him get inside and then gone out by another way with Mayo.

It was about then he heard the music.

It came softly, and in some strange way it was linked with color, so that Rick saw and heard it at the same time. The harmony was like the buildings. It was not born in a normal mind—normal, at least, by human standards. It came from everywhere, like the air. Rick supposed the system resembled a public address system of some kind, serving the whole city.

He could feel his brain crawling around in his skull, trying to hide.

The colors came stronger, pulsing like veils of mist through the eerie streets. They kept sliding off the edges of the spectrum into something else. They did things to the emotions, the nerves, even the intestinal functions. The music plucked at Rick's mind, stimulating it with notes and rhythms it was never meant to hear.

He began to think, suddenly, that he could understand the symbolic meanings of the buildings and where the curves led.

After that, for a while, he lost track of things, or very nearly. Some stubborn piece of his consciousness ran over the nightmare hills behind him, crying out, and nothing could stop it. Abruptly its cry got through to him and dragged him back, balanced delicately on a hairline between two worlds.

He was stark naked, and he was embracing a crystal pillar of no shape that he knew under the sun.

He sprang away from the pillar in shuddering nausea, clawing and clinging to his sanity.

"Wait," he thought. "Storm's doing this. He pushed a button somewhere to start this concert, like the guys that lived here used to do. He's looking in your mind and laughing to beat the devil, watching you fall apart. You going to let him laugh?"

Rick straightened up. That would mean Storm was still here, to be caught and killed. Things might yet work out.

Cords knotted up under the sweat on Rick's face. He pulled his strength, every bit of it, together, and sheathed his mind against the music and the colors. He started walking toward the nearest wall of the dome. He watched his feet and counted the steps, carefully, one by one.

If he were wrong, and Storm had gone away, it would mean disaster! But wait! He had to quit thinking things like that.

He reached the wall. He was not steady on his feet, but he was still counting. Far away along the curve he saw the steps again and went over and climbed them. Suddenly he realized that the hellish concert was over.

He sat down on the top step and waited until he had stopped shaking. Then he went into the next dome.

CHAPTER XIV

No BUILDINGS were here in this dome, no houses. In the center was a gigantic structure of metal and plastic. It hummed faintly, and a pale, shimmering radiance came out of it.

Ranged around it were row upon row of soft couches covered, coffin-like, with the transparent plastic. People lay upon them, either dead or asleep.

Rick could find no sign here of Storm and Mayo. He looked for the entrance to the dome beyond, found it, and started out across the floor.

The creatures under the plastic shields were not human. They were anthropoid but, somehow, in the texture of their flesh and the shape of their features, there was something alien. They lay quietly. If they breathed or stirred, Rick couldn't see it. But they were not dead, for their flesh was warm-looking and was not decayed.

He supposed that these were The Thinkers, who had built the city he had just left behind him. They seemed to be sexless. Their nude bodies were all alike. They had a perfection and beauty of form as unpleasant as their buildings.

Rick walked steadily toward the archway leading into the last of the three domes. He was not frightened. A man such as he came to the end of things, and one way or another, that was that. He looked around for a weapon, anything that could be used as one. There was nothing. He flexed his bandaged hands and went on.

131

There was no shelter, no cover of any kind around the steps and the archway. Rick did not try to hide. It was no use hiding from a telepath like Storm. What Rick wanted now was the finish, as quickly as possible. He wanted Storm.

There was no thought of death in his mind—for himself.

He climbed the stairway. He caught a glimpse of what looked like a vast laboratory and machine shop, and then Jaffa Storm was standing above him on the top step, his heavy blaster leveled at Rick's muscular body.

Rick stopped. Storm smiled at him, quite pleasantly.

"Where's Mayo?" asked Rick.

Storm jerked his head slightly, backward. "In there. She's quite safe. She won't be able to help you, and keep her that way. She's a wildcat." His black eyes looked Rick up and down. "Too bad you're going to miss the fun of seeing me break her."

Rick said nothing. His hands hung limp beside his naked thighs. His face was expressionless, his eyes veiled. He was halfway up the crystal steps, something less than his own height below Storm's feet.

"How did you like the concert?" Storm said.

Rick didn't answer.

Storm laughed. "Don't bother. I know. I was watching your mind every second." He indicated the sleepers beneath their coffin lids. "Curious tastes those birds had. I still don't know what they are or where they came from. I can't get through to their minds. I think that mentally they're not here any more, but have gone on into some realm of pure thought. The bodies, I think, are synthetic."

He broke off and stood studying Rick, as though

he wanted to impress every feature, every line on his memory.

"I never want to forget you," he said. "I have never before met a man I hated as much as I do you. I think I hate you because you're nearly as strong as I am, and that makes me afraid. I'm not used to being afraid. I don't like it."

"You've lost Mars," said Rick. "I took that from you."

"No," Storm said slowly. "No, you haven't. You messed up my plans, all right. You came blamed near killing me, too. Very smart of you to realize at the last minute that I had probably read your mind and would be ready for you. I was mighty busy, as you can imagine, and I didn't get the switch until it was too late to do anything but jump out of the way. As it was, I received a nasty cut from some flying metal, and my disintegrator was smashed to glory."

He swore abruptly, though, softly. "I wish I could think of a way to kill you that would really satisfy me."

Rick's mouth twisted in what was almost a lazy half-smile. "You can't kill me, Storm. This is my road, not yours."

Storm stared at him a moment. Then he laughed. "By Jupiter, you believe that, don't you?"

Rick nodded. "You knew I was coming."

"Yes. I kept track of the little one—what was her name, Kyra?—of her mind, until I knew she couldn't do me any harm, and I kept pretty close check on yours, too." He chuckled. "St. John and the Martian pulled a fast one on you, for fair! I always told that thick-headed Fallon he underestimated them."

Rick's eyes, after the mention of Kyra, had become deadly in a peculiarly cold way, as though no ordinary

133

human emotion could express what he felt. He still had not moved.

"But you've lost Mars," he repeated.

"No. That's the difference between us, Rick—the difference that's going to cost you everything. I trained my mind. It works for me, not I for it. When I found out what you were planning to do, uniting the Martians and the Earthmen against me, I knew you had a fair chance of succeeding. So I used my head.

"I'd been curious about the Thinkers for some time. The Martian seers, who might have discovered the truth, were forbidden to pry by their hereditary tabus. No Earthman had the power. But I did, and to blazes with tabus. I found out that the Thinkers thought-barrier—the mental compulsion felt by anyone trying to enter the domes—was merely a broadcast by a mechanism similar to a televisor. It was automatic, and gosh knows how long it's been running. I cut it off, of course, for your benefit.

"Anyway, after I forced my mind against that barrier, I found out that the Thinkers have simply— gone away. They're still alive, because I can feel the vibrations from their brains, but they've withdrawn somewhere beyond this world. I suppose they reached the point in their peculiar evolution where pure thought was the only unconquered realm left.

"But they left things behind them, Rick. An armory of weapons and machines such as men have dreamed of but never been able to produce. Disintegrators. Mental amplifiers. Energy projectors that make our Bannings look like children's toys. The Thinkers were named for a reason, you know. By gosh, I wish I knew what they were, where they came from! I'll hazard a guess, though. I think they were pre-human, and that their introverted culture was driven out by the appearance of man on the planet. So they built the domes, and that incredible city, and surrounded themselves with tabus, and lived peacefully in their own way.

"They went through a period of scientific invention that must have lasted an incredible number of years. Invention just for the kick of it, too. They never passed any of it on to humanity, and only used themselves what they needed for their own comfort. Like that dingus there."

Storm indicated the huge humming mechanism in the center of the dome.

"That warms them, feeds them by direct energy, keeps their bodies alive while their minds are playing around free in space and time," he said. Queer buried sparks came in his black eyes. "I wish I could follow them," he whispered, "for a little while."

Rick leaped forward, without warning.

He threw himself flat, clutching at Storm's ankles. It was the time he had waited for—the single second when Storm's mental attention was on something other than the brain of Richard Gunn Urquhart.

Storm's blaster beam flared obliquely, almost roasting the skin on Rick's back but not quite hitting him. Rick grasped the cloth of Storm's coverall and yanked with all his might. Storm fell back on his shoulder-blades, and the blaster let off a second time, at the top of the dome.

Rick's bare feet found traction on the steps and flung him forward again, his whole weight across Storm's body. The big man lost some more breath, and Rick clawed for the blaster.

The fall must have hurt Storm, but he didn't let it stop him. He used his free hand, and his knees, and his heavy boots. He was strong. Rick was a big man, and powerful, but Storm was stronger. He beat the living daylights out of Rick, but he couldn't shake him loose from that blaster.

Rick curled his naked body up, tightened his muscles, and took it. There was only one thing in the universe that mattered—the blaster. He got hold of Storm's thumb and worked, doggedly.

It broke. It tore out of the socket in a mess of ripped flesh and tendons, and Storm screamed like a wounded horse, and that was that. Rick had the blaster.

He broke away, to get off far enough to use it. One of Storm's boots took him squarely in the abdomen. Rick rolled back down the steps and lay there, trying to retch his insides out. The blaster skidded away across the crystal floor.

Storm got up. He looked at his hand. He pulled out his handkerchief and bound it tightly, using his teeth. Then he leaned against the wall of the arch and vomited.

At the foot of the steps, Rick was trying to get to his hands and knees, and sobbing aloud.

Storm noted where the blaster was. It had skittered far away, much farther away than Rick could hope to move for some time. Storm went down on the other side, into the laboratory dome.

Mayo McCall lay in the shelter of a machine too big and heavy for her to tip over. She was tied securely, and gagged. She needed no voice to tell Storm her thoughts. Her eyes told enough.

"You can kiss him good bye—what's left of him after I'm through," he whispered.

He found the small mechanism he was looking for, placed conveniently with others he had intended to take out to the 'copter after he was done with Rick. It was a harmless-looking little gadget—a shield over a prism inside a triangle of slightly luminous metal.

Storm wasn't sure how it worked. He guessed at cosmic ray frequencies, snared by the triangle and concentrated through the prism. But he knew what it would do.

He placed his left hand carefully behind the shield, his thumb over the control stud, and went back up the steps.

Rick had crawled to within ten feet of the blaster. Storm smiled. He pressed the stud. A little gossamer thread of radiance spun out from the prism. It touched the blaster. The metal crumbled to dust and then vanished.

"Rick—Ricky!" Storm said gently.

Rick turned his head. The great central machine hummed quietly, and the Thinkers dreamed their cosmic dreams, and paid no attention to the man who crouched naked on their floor, or the black giant who stood on their steps with destruction in his hands.

"You can't kill me," Rick whispered.

Storm laughed, without sound, and pressed the stud again.

Rick moved. When he found the strength in himself he never knew, except that it was that or die, and he wasn't ready to die. He rolled sideways. The beam missed him, eating a snaky groove in the floor. The outermost row of coffins were closed to him. He pulled himself behind the nearest one. They were solid to the floor. They offered cover, and though Storm could follow him mentally, he couldn't see to aim.

Rick started working back across the dome.

Storm followed them. He laced the coffins with the

crumbling light, leaving them ruined, the bodies within them partially destroyed. The Thinkers never stirred. Their minds were too far away, to be caring what happened to their flesh.

Rick played Storm with a sort of insane mixture of cleverness and sheer courage. He stayed behind each particular coffin until the beam had eaten dangerously close. Then he rolled or slid obliquely across the crystal floor, each time in a different direction, so that he was always screened except for an occasional second. Storm might have hit him, right handed. Left-handed, he couldn't.

Not at first, anyway. But Rick knew his luck couldn't hold forever. He felt like a plucked hen, with nothing in his hands, not even a rock.

His eyes blazed and narrowed suddenly. He began to circle, so that presently he would come back to the path they had already followed, where the ruined coffins were. Storm came doggedly after him. Storm was in no hurry. He was enjoying himself.

Rick came up to the coffin he wanted. It had been eaten away so that the plastic top was partly gone. The body inside was in two pieces now, cut cleanly through the middle. There was no blood, no viscera, no abdominal cavity. The flesh looked like sponge rubber.

Rick, crouched behind the coffin, reached up and took hold of the legs.

He waited a long moment, his brows knotted in concentration. Storm stood erect, smiling faintly, playing his disintegrator beam on Rick's shelter. Because of the arrangement of the coffins Storm's whole body was exposed to Rick's view if he looked over the top or around the right-hand end. From the left-hand end Storm's legs were hidden by the corner of another couch.

Rick whipped his unpleasant weapon down. It was lighter than human legs would have been, but heavy enough.

But Storm laughed, avoided it easily without taking his eyes from Rick's coffin. Suddenly he flicked the disintegrator beam upward, aiming above the right-hand corner.

At the same instant, Rick's head and shoulders thrust up and over the left-hand corner. He hurled the trunk section of the Thinker's synthetic body at Storm's head—and he did it left-handed.

Storm was slow, a fractional instant, caught off balance. The clumsy thing struck him. It was not heavy enough to stun him, or even do more than stagger him back against one of the coffins. But it was heavy enough to hamper him, and the dead arms went around him almost as though the reflexes still lived in their inhuman flesh.

Rick moved. He had never moved so fast in his life. Bruises, aches, weariness, the pain he carried with him—nothing mattered. He moved. He hit Storm before the carrion had slid free of his arm, or been shaken off.

Storm fired at Rick, but the beam went past him, and then Rick's hand chopped down edgewise across Storm's wrist and the deadly little prism dropped.

Rick got his bandaged hands where he had told Hugh St. John he wanted them.

He held them there, his eyes half-closed and happy, cat-like, long after there was any need. Storm didn't die easy, but he died.

"Instinct," whispered Rick conversationally to the

blackened face below his. "I'm left-handed. You didn't know that. You watched my mind figure out what I was going to do, and because you're right-handed you figured how it would be—only I'm left-handed. So you shot in the wrong place. Instinct crossed you up."

Storm didn't answer. He couldn't answer—now!

CHAPTER XV

YES, Storm was dead. But Rick didn't mention that to Mayo when he staggered into the laboratory dome and untied her. There aren't any words at a time like that. They clung to each other for a while, and Mayo cried a little, and Rick did too.

After a time, when the world had stopped swinging quite so wildly around them, Rick got up and began walking around, looking at the machines. He was a good mechanic. He was able to figure out what most of them were for, within reason. He was wearing Storm's black coverall. Storm's cigarettes were still in the breast pocket. Rick lighted one. His face was expressionless.

"What are you thinking, Rick?" Mayo said.

He didn't answer. Mayo got up and went slowly to the collection of mechanisms Storm had gathered together.

"He told me all about what happened," she said. "Hugh and Eran Mak will govern Mars well. Things will be good, if they're left alone to do what they've dreamed of."

Still Rick didn't answer.

Mayo picked up a small tube and aimed it at him.

"You can't have Mars," she said. "I won't let you have it, to play with."

He stood looking at her for a moment, with nothing in his eyes but a blank coldness.

"Yesterday I was in Caer Hebra," he said, as though to himself. "Kyra talked to me. I heard her."

Mayo was puzzled. She let the tube waver a little, and suddenly Rick was laughing at her.

"A tough baby, you are! And by Jaffrey, I'm not so sure you wouldn't use it, at that!" He turned away, blowing smoke at the lucid dome. "How do we get out of here?"

"I watched Storm. I know where the controls are. I can turn on the thought-projector, too, if we want to. But, Rick—what are you planning?"

"Don't you trust me?"

"No."

He went back to her.

"Now do you trust me?" he asked again, after a while.

"Less than ever. Oh Rick, won't you please—"

He stopped her words with his lips. "I haven't said anything, have I? Now let's clear out of this place."

Mayo's eyes held a cold doubt, but she nodded. Later, when she thought he wasn't looking, she slipped the tube into the pocket of her coverall.

"What about all this stuff?" she asked. "It's dangerous, Rick."

"It's been safe this long, I guess it'll keep a little longer. We'll pass the problem on to Mak and St. John and let them sweat about it."

"You're going to see them?"

"Yeah."

Rick reached into the pocket of his coverall and

pulled out the little energy projector Storm had used —the prism in the shining triangle. He turned the thing over in his hands, scowling at it, and then dropped it on the pile beside Mayo.

"Where's the control, honey?"

"For this dome, it's over there on the left. Or do you want to go back through the city?"

"No," he said. "I do not want to go back through the city." Mayo went away. When she came back he put his arm around her shoulders as they crossed the dome to the hidden entrance.

They took the fuel from Storm's 'copter and carried it to Rick's and took off. Presently Rick noticed that Mayo was crying quietly.

"What's wrong?"

"I was thinking of Kyra. Storm told me all about it. He would. I'm glad you could be with her."

"Yeah," said Rick. "Yeah, she died happy."

They sighted pursuing ships several times, but nothing could stay with them. Rick lapsed into a sullen, brooding silence and snarled at Mayo every time she tried to speak. Finally she gave it up. She sat with her eyes closed, and a couple of grim, tight lines hardened into the corners of her mouth.

Presently Rick turned on his transmitter and got in touch with the Company. The switchboard operator goggled at him and then began pushing plugs frantically. In a couple of seconds Hugh St. John was looking out of the screen at Rick, with Eran Mak behind his shoulder.

They both saw Mayo at the same time, and came crowding against the screen as though they wanted to get through to her. Especially St. John. Rick watched him sourly. "That guy's crazy about her," he thought. "He's so crazy about her his blood's almost tepid. The lily!"

They hardly noticed Rick at first, until Mayo had told about Storm and the Polar Cities, and what Rick did there. Then St. John turned to him.

"I'm glad you came back," he said gravely.

"That's fine," Rick answered. "You made it so easy for me, too."

"We did what we thought was right, Rick."

"That explains it okay, then," snarled Rick. "It whitewashes the whole thing. Doesn't matter what you do to a guy as long as you think it's right. Right for whom, St. John? And if you say 'Mars' I'll beat your head off as soon as I land."

St. John's mouth tightened. Behind him Eran Mak smiled and nodded. His golden eyes were bright.

"I never thought of you as a chicken, Rick," he said. "But here you come, home to roost. Too bad you have Mayo with you. I've got a feeling it would be much simpler just to shoot you down over the field."

"Uh huh," Rick said. "That's one reason I have her with me." The bells tinkled faintly in the Martian's ears, and Rick shuddered. "You better tell all those MPP boys to clear the air for me. I'm coming down."

"Better make it the landing field," St. John said. "You ruined the 'copter deck in the compound. We'll send a car for you."

"And an armed escort?"

"And an armed escort."

"I'm coming in peace," said Rick. "How I go out again is something you can worry about then."

St. John gave him a cold and level look, and nodded. The screen went dead. Mayo leaned back in her seat again and closed her eyes.

"Rick," she said quietly. "I love you. I'll go anywhere with you, do anything with you, except one thing. Think about it. Think hard, before you do anything."

"I've done nothing else but think, for a long time," Rick said.

They didn't speak after that. Rick swooped in to the old Company field where he had stolen the ship that wrecked Storm's plans, and made his landing. A car was waiting for them, with an escort of jeeps manned by Martian Government men. Rick submitted quietly to a polite but thorough search. They found no weapon on him. They did not search Mayo.

The car sped smoothly away toward the compound. Rick glanced up at the distant towers of Ruh on the cliffs above the sea-bottom, and his eyes were as cold and depthless as amber glass.

Martian G-men, mostly soft-muscled political office-holders, ushered them into the building St. John was using in place of the now non-existent Administration Pylon. St. John met them at the door of the office and persuaded the escort to go away. They didn't want to. They looked at Rick much as the men of Valkis had, but for a different reason. On the face of it they were outraged by the supposed sacrilege to the Collar of Ruh. In reality, they were worried about the new Union Government and what it was going to do to their jobs.

They did go away, however, leaving Rick and Mayo alone with St. John and Eran Mak. The Martian was lounging in his habitual position on the window sill, smoking and swinging the bells back and forth in his ear with a monotonous forefinger. He watched Rick through the smoke, his eyes yellow and unwinking as a hawk's.

St. John took Mayo in his arms. Rick turned away irritably, not wanting to see either of their faces. He let them talk, a few low words, while he sprawled out wearily in a big chair and got a cigarette going. He felt suddenly as old as Mars, and as tired.

"There are no words to thank you, Rick," St. John said presently. "This is a very strange situation. I'm grateful to you with all my heart, and yet I wish you weren't here. I'm afraid of you, and afraid of what may have to be done."

"At least you're honest about it," Rick said.

"There's no point in deception." St. John sat down behind a desk piled high with papers. He looked at the mess and sighed. "Forming a new government out of what we have to work with is no easy job. I've been over to Kahora several times, and Mak's been wearing his legs off running back and forth to Martian headquarters. I've stayed here because it seemed to be the focal point of all the trouble and I thought I could handle things better if I did. Also, the Company had to be taken care of. My heavens, the things Storm had been doing!"

Rick glanced almost lazily at St. John. "Yeah. You haven't got recognition and charter yet from the Interplanetary Authority, have you?"

"Not yet. But there's no question that we will, considering the circumstances."

"That is, all the circumstances but one," replied Rick.

St. John nodded slowly. "That's what you came back for, isn't it?"

Rick jumped up. "My stars!" he roared. "What did you think I'd do? Who did all this anyway. Who was it sweated in these cursed mines, and took the beatings and the burnings and the kicks in the teeth?" He thrust his hands out. The bandages had come off, showing the raw new scars. "Was it you got pinned to the wall in Ruh, or me? Was it you that Beudach put the Collar on, or me? Was it you that talked to the Marshies and the Earthmen into fighting together, into being blood brothers from here on out? Was it you stuck your neck out there in the Thieves' Quarter, maybe to get a knife in it, and was it you stole that ship and crashed it on top of Jaffa Storm?"

His voice was making the windows rattle. His face was blank and hard with fury, the veins like whipcords on his temples. He stopped suddenly and paced back and forth a little, and when he spoke again his voice was only a tight whisper.

"By jumping jingoes, I've given too much, St. John," he said. "Blood and sweat and the fear of dying, while you were sitting on your hands, wishing. If you and Eran Mak think you can get rid of me with a crack on the head and fifty thousand credits to show for it, you're crazy!" He laughed and swung around so he could face both of them. "Would you be satisfied, St. John? Would you, Mak?"

There was a long silence. Eran Mak smoked quietly, enigmatic as the sea-bottom outside.

"No, I don't suppose I would be," St. John said slowly, at last.

"The question," said Eran Mak, "is not whether you're satisfied, but whether or not you can do anything about getting satisfied."

Rick smiled.

"Tell 'em, about what's up there under the Polar domes, and what Storm was going to do with it," he said to Mayo.

She told them. But her eyes, like Eran Mak's, were on Rick.

He gave them plenty of time to think it over. They didn't like it. The thought of all that power frightened them. St. John reached out once for the telescreen, and stopped.

"No, I wouldn't trust the Marshies that far just yet, if I were you," Rick said with a laugh. "All right, so there's force there. But I don't have to use it."

"May I remind you you're a prisoner here," Mak said.

"Sure. So was I on the *Mary Ellen Dow*. A guy goes through a certain number of things, and he gets so he doesn't care any more. Like I said, I don't have to use it."

He was close behind Mayo now. Quite suddenly he caught her around the neck with one arm and held her while he snatched the tube out of the pocket where she had hidden it. Then he let her go and stepped back.

He aimed the tube at a chair. A little pink tongue licked out and touched it, and there was nothing but a heap of dust.

"Disintegrator," said Rick. "Now, maybe you'd better get busy with the telescreen. A planet-wide hook-up, see? Maybe you'd better tell everybody just what happened here the night of the raid."

Mayo got up slowly and stood facing him.

"You know what that will mean," St. John said.

"Sure. Your geese will be pretty well fried, won't they? The fine altruistic saviors of Mars won't look so hot, will they?"

"Think a minute, Rick, before you do this," St. John said. "Men fight any way they can to win what

147

they want. Believe it or not, Mak and I are honest. You have fifty thousand credits, remember."

"Not any more. They bought my way off the *Mary Ellen Dow*."

Eran Mak whistled. "So it meant that much to you!" He slid off the sill and stood up. "What will you take in place of Mars?"

"What could you give me in place of a world?" countered Rick.

They stood looking at him, St. John and Mayo and Eran Mak. He scowled, his jaw set stubbornly, his eyes hooded and sulky. He was careful that he should not see Mayo's face.

St. John sighed. He reached out, slowly like an old man, to press the connection on the telescreen.

"Wait!" Rick said hoarsely.

They stiffened, staring at him. There was sweat on his face and his hand trembled slightly.

"Wait," he said. "Listen. Yesterday Kyra died in Caer Hebra. She died smiling. She said she'd live again, in the new Mars, and remember that she helped make it. Helped make it—with me! And by Jaffrey, I did do it! I pulled this messy dustball together and made it tick. Nobody else could have done it. Nobody but me!"

He paused and rubbed his hand over his eyes. "I don't know why I give a cuss what Kyra said. I don't know whether she'll live again, or remember. But if she did— Oh, rats! Mayo, come here."

She came. There was a glow starting back in her eyes.

"Listen, Mayo. Is this what the prophecy meant, my shadow over Mars? The shadow that's there now and will always be there, because I put Mars together

148

with my two hands? I've been thinking, Mayo. I can get this world, or at least I can make a blamed good try at it. I can milk it dry, maybe, but—well, there are other worlds, and I'm young yet, and I—" He pulled her close to him. "Does that make sense, Mayo?" I'd rather have you than Mars. Like I told you once, you're part of me, and if I couldn't have you, I wouldn't care what else I had. You know something? All the time I was getting away to come back here, I wasn't really thinking of Mars. I was thinking of you."

"I said you had a soul, if you could ever find it," Mayo whispered.

Rick put his lips on hers. "Bosh, for my soul. I found you." His arms tightened.

St. John and Erak Mak turned away.

"Other worlds," Rick murmured after a while. "There's always Outside—the Belt, and even Jupiter. Ships get better every year, and they need trail-breakers out there. Unless you want to stay here, without me."

She stopped his lips with hers.

Rick started to laugh. "I guess I'm crazy. Looking at St. John over there, behind that desk all stacked up with papers, already getting bags under his eyes worrying about politics and charters and chiselling bums, I'm glad I don't have to. I got to thinking about that, too. Breaking trail is fine, but building the road afterward is just a lot of hard work, and somebody else can have it."

He moved forward, holding Mayo tight in his arm. "Okay, you guys. You've got the grief. But don't think I'm through blackmailing you. I'm sticking you for the best blamed ship that flies, all fitted up, and a

149

crew to match, and first trade rights for what I bring in from the Belt. And listen." His voice dropped and he flushed uncomfortably.

"Just in case Kyra does come back—build a good road, will you? I'd kind of like her to remember me and think that my shadow over Mars was still a good one."

FRITZ LEIBER

06218	The Big Time $1.25
30301	Green Millennium $1.25
53330	Mindspider $1.50
76110	Ships to the Stars $1.50
79152	Swords Against Death $1.25
79173	Swords and Deviltry $1.50
79162	Swords Against Wizardry $1.25
79182	Swords in the Mist $1.25
79222	The Swords of Lankhmar $1.25
95146	You're All Alone 95¢

Available wherever paperbacks are sold or use this coupon.

WINNER OF THE HUGO AWARD AND THE NEBULA AWARD FOR BEST SCIENCE FICTION NOVEL OF THE YEAR

*04594 Babel 17 Delany $1.50
*05476 Best Science Fiction of the Year Del Rey $1.25
06218 The Big Time Leiber $1.25
*10623 **City** Simak $1.75
16649 The Dragon Masters Vance $1.50
16704 Dream Master Zelazny $1.50
19683 The Einstein Intersection Delany $1.50
24903 Four For Tomorrow Zelazny $1.50
47071 The Last Castle Vance 95¢
47803 Left Hand of Darkness Leguin $1.95
72784 Rite of Passage Panshin $1.50
79173 Swords and Deviltry Leiber $1.50
80694 This Immortal Zelazny $1.50

Available wherever paperbacks are sold or use this coupon.

Ursula K. Le Guin

10703	City of Illusion	$1.75
47803	Left Hand of Darkness	$1.95
66953	Planet of Exile	$1.25
73293	Rocannon's World	$1.50

Available wherever paperbacks are sold or use this coupon.

33I